Rendezvous

Novel By
ASHISH JAIN

RG
books

Published By

Redgrab Books Pvt. Ltd.

942, Mutthiganj, Prayagraj, 211003
www.redgrabbooks.com
contact@redgrabbooks.com

Price in india : 225/- INR

First published by Redgrab Books in 2023
Copyright © 2023 Redgrab Books Pvt. Ltd.
Copyright Text © 2023 Ashish Jain
Printed and bound in India
Cover Design & Typesetting by Redgrab Books team
ISBN : 978-93-95697-22-4

DEDICATION

I dedicate this book to all those people who
had loved someone purely

FOREWORD

Neither am I a writer nor do I possess enough skill to compose stories. But yes, sometimes I scribble for no specific reason, or rather I set out on a journey of aimless thoughts, and whatever I feel along the way or whatever is retained by my memory, I mold it in words and narrate it.

Before writing, I pondered quite a bit about the way this story should be told. Should it be written from the perspective of one character or should more than one character be used as a medium to convey the core thought. Ultimately, I decided to keep the story free from any boundaries of form.

The choice of language too consumed a major part of my thinking space. Should it be Hindi - my mother tongue or English – the language I use in my work-related correspondence? But since my realm of imagination, the language in which thoughts were taking birth in my mind, the conversations between characters and all those characters were rooted in Hindi environment, it was only logical that this story should be written in Hindi. And so, it was originally written in Hindi. This book in your hand, is its English edition.

Every individual has his / her own experiences springing out of their lives. Some end up as stray moments, some perish, some go on to sow seeds of new stories, while traveling relentlessly across the terrain of life. While reading this story, it's up to you to decide whether my journey has concluded or if I have reached somewhere. However, I believe that stories can be conceived only when the journey is continuous.

I sometimes wonder how eccentric that moment must have been when the first story took birth. Who must have woven a story for the first time? How must have it been? Was the protagonist based on the writer himself or did he choose to write about someone else or did that forgotten writer ever feature in someone else's story? Even back then, did the transformation of characters follow the changing of seasons over the course of the story?

As time passed, some stories were treasured, while many got lost. But I am sure, one thing is still the same as it must have been while writing or telling the story back then. The amalgamation of moods that reflect in the storyteller's expressions while he is in the act of narrating - a little relaxed, a little ticklish and a calming smile. This feeling must have remained the same over all these centuries.

Every story leaves us under its spell. To some it may feel like their own tale. To some it may be a gateway into a world of new ideas and concepts. Some may discover new realizations in it, or some may unknowingly get emotionally attached to a character. I have tried to tell a story that I hope, is able to cast a similar spell, and if it manages to touch your heart, then it will be safe for me to believe that this journey of words has found its destination.

Ashish
January 21, 2022

If an individual who leads life in a specific routine, is perceived as boring or monotonous, then such adjectives fit well to that lifestyle.

At the core of his lifestyle was his insistence to live on his own terms and to remain lost in his own world. I believe, there are diverse ways of assessing one's personality. However, on a personal level, you may think of him as a selfish person. Even though all this was true about him, he came across as a sensible, social, and a friendly person despite his selfishness or whatever more there was to him.

The fact that he had gone through many ups and downs in life, may have something to do with his personality being molded in such a peculiar way. Nobody's life remains a virgin from experiences of success and failure, but this ratio was much wider in his life. Countable successes and countless failures had mentored and thus enriched him.

The impression that his life was full of thorns, would be as erroneous as an assumption that it was as good as everyone else's. However, gauging by his present state of being, his present at the time this story began seemed better than his past.

'Belonging to a middle-class family' comes with a set of advantages and disadvantages - such as there is no immediate need to cut-down on everyday necessities, but often there is no shortage of necessities either.

His childhood too was spent with focus on a few necessities and many needs that mostly remained unfulfilled. So, while growing up and studying in an environment composed with limited resources, the tendency of enjoying his solitude, even while living with family, gradually took shape within his being. An average student who had completed his studies with multiple pauses, while fighting various problems that kept sprouting in his path. His desire towards further studies felt practically unachievable due to memories of bitter experience and various challenges of his past. He had made peace with the thought that perceiving further studies was as good as a trying to eat a rotten pudding. Therefore, he had kept his student life on pause after completing his engineering.

Since one doesn't secure a job just because one doesn't hail from the 'creamy layer' or more importantly one doesn't fall on the right side of the margin popularly known as 'cut off', he had to return home and establish base there, where new challenges awaited him. While struggling to get a job, he met some new people. New friendships were forged, which brought new experiences, which in turn opened doors to explore new curiosities. In a beat of this rhythm, one and a half years were spent, and his job search kept going on and on. At that point, seeking a job was his only job.

His days and nights were being pulled by a thread of just one hope – that some *jugaad'* or some help will present a chance for him to establish a steady source of income, which will help him reduce the burden on his family.

Every day the same staring eyes used to ask him -

"So, brother, what are your plans?"

Or

"So-n-So went to So-n-So place to do So-n-So job? What's happening with you?"

Or some people with a mature expression -

"One day or another you will get a job, right? It's just a matter of time. Maybe your time isn't right as of now."

One day he left his house with a heart full of determination. He waved farewell to his months of struggle with a lucrative offer letter in his hand.

Being a programmer by profession, he had begun to relish his hard-earned but small job, in a small company, by fulfilling his responsibilities of his small post. The new sun of a brand-new technological era had just risen and had only moved a few inches of its long sprint. A job in this new white-collar sector of Software companies brought along a certain 'Dignity' to the job holders wherever they went in social circles.

However, he was constantly aware that there was nothing special in him and his work, that he should be praised with words like 'Exceptional' or 'Brilliant'. But he knew how to conclude and present his work in the best way possible. One of his defining characteristics was that he would answer everything with pauses, taking time to think thoroughly about every topic, and this was not liked or rather misunderstood by many. Yet, in midst of these habitual pauses, life kept moving forward smoothly.

He fit perfectly in category of people who tend to make few friends. Now this doesn't elongate his list of enemies. In fact, there was almost no one whom he could count as enemies. If his peculiarly serious ways of life didn't make him an easy-going friend, in the very least he had earned quite a few well-wishers for himself.

Despite being loaded with work as compared to his low salary, there was a kind of comfort, which kept him pursuing each day with a belief, that his next day will be even better. Since that era was still secure from the slavery of smart phones, he had enough free time to read books. He balanced his time between Hindi and English literature, which filled his empty life to some extent. Time spent with our own selves gives us immense inner happiness. He felt the same way whenever he had a book in his hand.

Twenty-six springs of reading poetry had passed, but he had not yet developed a fondness for the tenderness that poems hold in themselves. When it came to scope, poetry and songs had a limitation of portraying nothing much other than short, fragile moments. Most of the time, he found himself confused in this matter. His eagerness to find pleasure in poetry, met strong resistance from his practical reasoning. Thus, he remained untouched by literature.

He was an average looking guy, of medium stature, fair complexion, and body of average proportion - neither fat nor lean, but all those factors were redeemed by the sparkle in his deep black eyes, which were always seeking something, hurling curious questions at everything, expressing feelings where his tongue failed.

Apart from literature, he had developed a distinct interest in films and theatre. Distinct because, his choice of films deviated from the usual blockbuster cinema and bloomed in the realm of artistic, evocative films, that were demanding in terms of patience and left him with a lot of food for thought and nuanced feelings. Similarly, his choice of music too was offbeat, as he was quite finicky about the tunes, he would allow his life to be filled with - either playing on his phone or humming from his lips.

Whenever he was in his own zone, a song would flow in his voice – as melodious as it sounded effortless.

He had a natural tendency to observe things. He would leisurely stand by the window of his room for hours, watching people walking through the streets below and try to imagine what they might be talking about or would wonder what might be going on in the mind of a solitary stranger. Sometimes if he woke up in the middle of the night, he would look down from his window to see if there was someone he could observe and would wait there, until his sleep returned to dominate him.

Dawn used to be the most special time of his day. When his side of the world was still in bed, he would go for a walk to a nearby park to steal those tranquil moments from the city and bury them deep in his chest. The calmly rising sun reminded him of himself.

Akash was passing through life peacefully, at his own speed, creating his own paths, engrossed in himself, living each day as it came.

***

One Saturday morning in the month of June, Akash was sitting in his room, sipping a steaming cup of tea and his eyes were gliding through the newspaper. His expressions kept changing every now and then, like giggling clouds tease the sky. His eyes were staring at the newspaper, but his mind was chasing something else.

He had rented a room in a large two-storeyed building, in which he had composed his space to meet his solitary lifestyle. Some other working people like him had rented apartments in that hostel. The window of his first-floor room opened to a view of the street. The fresh morning air felt like it would wash over his face and fill up his room. Every day, a beam of sunlight would pierce the skylight window and scatter across his room.

Holding on to his ongoing thought, his eyes took flight from the newspaper as he took a deep breath, reclining on the chair, tenderly observing the sunrays filtering through the skylight. Then he closed his eyes and sat there for a while. He was deeply immersed in his thoughts when his phone rang. Prakhar's number flashed on the screen. Before he could decide between answering or disconnecting, the phone went silent on its own. However, Prakhar's number appeared on the screen again. This time he answered without hesitation and uttered gently -

"Say dear, how are you?"

"Bro, where are you?" Prakhar asked in his Gujarati 'accent'.

"I'm in my room," he replied softly.

"Listen, if you are free, then let's go for a walk. What do you say?" Prakhar asked.

"Where do you want to go so early in the morning?" Akash asked.

"Come-on buddy, get ready soon. Breakfast is on me." Prakhar replied in his bright voice.

"Oh yeah! What's the matter with you? You woke up so early just to feed me!" The clock was showing Eight o' clock, which seemed too early for someone like Prakhar to be awake and ready to step out of his house.

Akash's sarcasm was sliced by a giggling reply, "This is my usual time to begin the day. You tell me, are you coming or not?"

"I can't go, man!" Akash said.

"You have to. If I am awake in the morning, don't you think there must be something special? Otherwise, why would I have offered to treat you with breakfast?"

When Akash did not give any answer for a while, he again said - "Come-on bro, please!"

Akash replied in brief, "Hmm, okay."

"See you in half n' hour. Get ready quickly." Saying so, Prakhar hung up the phone.

He had been receiving such impulsive offers from Prakhar earlier too. Whenever he had to ask strange questions or share gossip notes on a scandal, he could not resist narrating the whole fleshed out version of events by taking him to a park or a restaurant. Assuming the same was to be expected today as well, Akash entered the bathroom to take a bath.

Akash was standing near the gate below the hostel. He was gazing across the road, when Prakhar pulled up his bike in front of him. Akash signaled him to wait and bought some bubblegum from the nearby grocery store and then got on his bike.

Placing his hand on Prakhar's shoulder for balance, he asked – "Tell me now, what's the matter?"

Prakhar said through his helmet - "Let's go to the coffee house and we will talk there!"

"Okay let's go!" Saying so, Akash busied himself chewing on his bubblegum.

After a twenty minutes ride, the bike stopped in front of a coffee house. Akash spit the bubblegum in a garbage can and turned towards Prakhar, "Is there anything special?"

While parking the car, Prakhar said, "Yes, you may take it that way."

Both took their favorite corner in the café and gestured to the waiter with their hands.

"So, our usual order?" Akash asked.

"Yes, a plate of cutlets and tea for me. Masala dosa and coffee for you, right?" Prakhar asked while fidgeting with his finger.

"Hmm…" Akash approved. "So, now tell me, which Epic you want to narrate today?"

"Arrey, no epic n stuff. I have something serious going on." Prakhar said cleaning his spectacles with his handkerchief.

"Serious, what do you mean?" Akash asked.

"You know Shefali from the finance department, right?" Prakhar asked, rolling his eyes.

"Yeah, I know!" Akash shook his head.

"Dude, she has been stealing glances at me since a few days. Those kind of glances… You know what I mean?" He said with a wink.

"Yeah, so you think she has hots for you?" Akash asked with a laugh.

"What else! Otherwise, why would she look at me that way? She has never ever spoken to me directly. And nowadays she makes it a point to greet me in passing." Prakhar's eyes were shining as he spoke.

"You mean, the rest of the girls don't greet you in passing?" Akash said, looking straight into his eyes.

"Hey, they do, man…" Prakhar's sentence got abruptly cut by Aakash's taunt, "…but the tone of her greetings is a bit different; Isn't it?"

                                                    Rendezvous

"Yes, dude!" He said with a broad smile.

"Hmm then what next?" Akash asked rolling his eyes.

"Propose her..." Prakhar said, crossing his fingers.

"Are you telling me or asking?" Akash asked while keeping his phone on the table.

"Of-course, I am asking, dude! What should I do? Tell me." Prakhar asked, shaking Akash's hand vigorously.

"Don't you think you're being too hasty to jump on conclusions?" Akash asked.

"No bro, she has been looking at me for more than a month now and she doesn't have a boyfriend as far as I know. That's why I am wondering if I should propose her tomorrow over a call."

The waiter had just begun serving their food when the word 'Propose' perked up his ears. He stared at both in turn and then left. Akash asked, "Why? Is there some sort of auspicious time tomorrow? And why over the phone?"

"I feel it is safe on the phone. In case things go wrong, the intensity of any potential insult is considerably reduced" Prakhar said baring his teeth.

"Your choice, bro." Akash said raising his eyebrows. Then he joined his palms and asked, "When you have already decided, why are you dragging me into all this?"

"Bro, I will need your help tomorrow?" Leaning towards Akash, spreading his chest on the table, Prakhar said as if whispering, "She talks to you, man. It would be great if you call her and then give the phone to me"

"Listen dude! Keep me away from this whole thing," said Akash, staring at him.

"Dude, if you don't help me in this, who else will? I am relying on your support. Please, please!" Prakhar said, tugging at Akash's hand.

Pulling his hand back, Akash asked in a disinterested tone, "Okay, but what can I possibly say to her?"

"All you have to say is that Prakhar wants to talk to you and then give the phone to me. I'll take care of the rest."

"Ok, Ok. Then come over to my place tomorrow. Let's see what we can do."

"Thanks man! Prakhar said widening his eyes.

“Come on, then finish your breakfast and get out of here,” said Akash, pushing him back.

"Why? Aren't you coming along?" Prakhar asked while fixing his hair.

“No” Akash replied, “I will sit here for a bit and then go to the public library and browse through books.”

After finishing the breakfast, Prakhar left. Akash sat there for a while, then walked out of the coffee house and walked all the way to the library. Today being the first day of the weekend, he wanted to borrow a good book from the library and consume it with relish in his room.

Akash had lost the track of time as the book took over his senses. It was already past twelve in the noon when he raised his eyes towards the clock. There was nothing else to do during the day, so he got ready and went to a cyber cafe across the street. There he camped in front of a computer to check his e-mails. A few days ago, he had given an interview in a company and was waiting for a response from the HR. After having skimmed through all the mails, when he did not see any reply, he closed his mailbox and opened Yahoo Messenger.

Chatting applications were the new trend during those days. The youth had embraced this new way of communication not just due to the novelty factor, but also due to the convenience it presented. Many times, Akash would chat with his old friends. He entered his family group and was looking up and down the list when he got a message from a user, “Hi!”

The username was neither poetic, nor aping a Bollywood or Hollywood personality, neither different just for the sake of being different, not indicative of the gender of the person on the other side. At that time, such arrangements were a boon for youngsters, which offered the potential to fulfill both their explicit as well as hidden desires to some extent. A few time-pass relationships were forged while some relationships were limited to a single conversation.

Neither had Akash responded till now, nor was there any further typing from the other end. His attention was on the message that had flashed on his phone –

"Where are you from?" The mysterious user asked further.

Akash had not yet made up his mind to give any reply. Still, twitching one corner of his lips slightly to form a dimple on his cheek, he replied -"India"

"I mean, which place in India?" The unknown user enquired.

Akash replied - "Bangalore"

"Oh!" Seeing that word, Akash felt this will probably be the last message from this stranger. What can one make out from a reply like "Oh"? Did it mean to convey disappointment? Or was it meant to convey surprise? Or did it mean nothing - just a reply for the sake of it – an expressionless "Oh"?

He sat there for a while and then as soon as he was about to get up, the next message appeared - "I am from Nainital."

Nainital – the word sent a cool gust of breeze humming melodiously by his ears and he almost shivered. He replied - "Oh ho! Green valleys, floating clouds. By the way, I do not hail from Bangalore. I am a North Indian."

"Okay…" came the reply "…then where are you from? Do you work in Bangalore?

Akash still had no clarity about the gender of the other person from this small conversation. But one thing was clear - that the other person was only interested in 'normal' conversation. So, Akash also went on to write -"Yes, I work in a software company. I belong to a small town in Madhya Pradesh."

"Okay" the screen flashed.

Again 'Okay'! This is most probably her / his catchphrase. Akash thought with a smirk.

There was a pause on the exchange of messages from both the sides. Akash looked at the clock which was about to strike One. He was just about to get off the chair and head back to his room, when the next message arrived, "I teach at a college here in Nainital. I joined a few months ago."

Akash sat back and read the message. Something about the message gave an aura of femineity to the stranger he had been interacting with, "Oh Okay…" he replied immediately.

A smiling 'smiley' and a waving hand flew in from the other side and perched on the screen.

"You are teasing me with my own words?"

A slight smile appeared on Akash's lips and then he wrote - "Oh no, you need not think that way. I wrote it just the way I thought."

"I know" she replied.

Then there was silence for a while… Wondering what the stranger on the other side must be feeling and thinking, Akash couldn't help looking at the clock which had just struck One, as hunger had already invaded his senses, so he typed, "I have to leave for my lunch now..." As soon as he was about to press enter, another message popped up on his screen, "May I know your name?"

Now leaving at this point would make him look rude, which he had no intention of making her feel, and there was no risk in sharing names either, so he typed, "Akash". Then he crossed his hands and sat back on the chair. This time he wanted to see what kind of reply comes from there and in how much time. He didn't have to wait much

"Avni… That's what they call me." Came her reply.

"Quite a unique name!" Akash typed.

"My parents must have been thoughtful about it." She typed from there.

After a while there was silence, during which Akash thought why he had faked the feeling of wonder over the name, as it wasn't a new name for him and nothing special seemed to be happening right now. Moreover, his hunger was getting the better of him, so he sent his earlier message.

" I must leave for my lunch now. See you soon."

"Oh well, goodbye then. Nice meeting you" her reply came up immediately.

After typing "Same here." Akash closed the chat and left the cybercafe.

He entered his room, picked up his book again and dived head down in the well of words and soon dozed off while the book slowly slept on his chest.

Some things that occur for the first time among strangers - most are formal and very few that can be bookmarked for remembrance, and many are insignificant. The interaction between Akash and Avni too was an awkwardly formal one. There wasn't much to be remembered. But sometimes destiny takes you on unusual paths, which you enter without expectations, but you unknowingly begin doing things as are written for your journey, as if it were an instance of divine providence. Due to which the first thing that came to Akash's mind as soon as he opened his eyes was the memory of those words on his screen in that cybercafé, "Avni… That's what they call me.".

And as he was still coming back to his senses, that chat screen swirled in front of his eyes.

"Oh well, goodbye then. Nice meeting you"

"Same here."

He got up with a jolt. Sitting in the same posture for a while, he looked at the clock which was now about to strike four. Raising his arms upwards, he started humming a forgotten Hindi song,

'gungunaati huyi ek nadee mil gayi

ajnabee sheher mein dosti mil gayi

tum miley kya mujhe, zindagi mil gayi'

the river was humming when i found her

unknown was the city where i found a friend

when we met, it felt as if life had found me

The song was still on his lips when Prakhar's message appeared on the phone screen "Bro, tomorrow at ten o'clock, I will come to your place and then we will call Shefali. Ok?"

"Okay" replied Akash, and threw the phone aside, then picked up the book and again lost himself in its pages.

***

There was something different about this Sunday morning. It had a distinctive glow, and a light breeze was flowing leisurely, sunrays were filtering through the trees, the leaves flying around casually in the street, the melodious voice of birds and a strange feeling tugging at the heart.

Akash's gaze was resting on a few jasmine flowers in front of him. He went near the flowers and touched their petals as if he wanted to capture and store their tenderness on the skin of his fingers. A mellow smile warmed up his face, as he covered it with his palms, as if under an urge to drink all the fragrance. He stood silently in that relaxed position for a while, then uncovered his face, and slowly opened his eyes. The view in front of him had renewed itself through this magical fragrance. He felt a peculiar lightness in his limbs, as if he could even fly if he wanted to. He walked slowly towards his room, still trying to absorb as much of this exquisite beauty as possible.

Soon Akash had settled back in his Sunday routine, when Prakhar called. He realized that it was ten o'clock already. Prakhar's voice came from the other end, "Bro, I am coming in a while. You're in the room, aren't you?"

Akash remembered that today he must call Shefali and help Prakhar in driving his love story to conclusion. He replied, "Yes, I am the room. Come over." and disconnected the phone.

Akash took a quick bath and was getting ready, when Prakhar entered the room and sat on the bed with a jerk.

"What's up, Romeo?" Akash asked with a chuckle.

Prakhar stared at him for a moment and replied - "How would you know the addictive tortures of this sweet pain that come with matters of the heart?" Then dancing his eyes dramatically like a Hindi film hero, he added, "Dude, she has stolen sleep from my eyes. I wasn't able to sleep for a single minute last night."

Akash laughed hearing his fake tone and that filmi dialogue. With a teasing chuckle, he said, "And I do not know what all you are going to lose further. Hope you have prepared yourself for all that."

Prakhar replied in mock irritation, and with a little pinch of boldness, "Yes, you don't have to worry about all that. I'll deal with it. Just call her and hand over the phone to me.

Akash nodded his head, handing over his phone to Prakhar, asked him to type Shefali's number. Prakhar dialed and handed over the phone to Akash with a pleading tone, "Bro, it's all in your hands now."

                                              Rendezvous

Blinking both eyes slowly, Akash gave him a comforting look, as he placed the phone on his ear. Akash, seated himself on the chair, listening to the phone ringing, tapping his fingers of the other hand on the table. Within a few seconds, a voice came from the other end, "Hello!"

"Hi" Akash replied, looking into Prakhar's eyes which were staring nervously back at him.

"Akash here." Akash replied.

"Oh! Hi Akash, how are you?" Shefali asked.

"Fit and fine! How about you?" Akash asked in a low voice.

"Doing good" then she paused and asked, "How did you remember me of all people on a Sunday?"

"Just like that" Akash replied directly, then paused for a while and added "Are you at home right now?"

"Yes! Why? What happened?" Shefali asked.

"Nothing happened yet, but I guess, it may happen any time soon." and he smiled with mischief in his voice. By now Prakhar's wide stare was making him look like an owl.

"Well… Listen…" Akash got up and came out of the room while simultaneously gesturing Prakhar to stay seated.

From the lofty bed, he could watch Akash moving outside, talking to Shefali animatedly, his hands swinging expressively in the air. The conversation went on that way for a couple of minutes, after which Akash made a gesture with his hand calling Prakhar to the balcony. Prakhar's eyebrows were dancing in panic when he came out, "What happened, bro?"

"She is on the phone. Ask her." Saying so, Akash put the phone on Prakhar's palm and hurriedly inside the room.

Reclining on his bed, he looked outside in the balcony. Prakhar could be seen speaking less vigorously and shaking his head more. This went on for about ten minutes, after which Prakhar came back to the room, hurling his lifeless body in the chair, taking a deep breath, he looked at Akash who was smiling, then laughing loudly, sat up in his bed and asked, "What happened, son? Is everything okay?"

Pulling at his hair, Prakhar asked, "You already knew, didn't you?" And he flung towards Akash.

Akash, defended himself, and made him sit on the bed saying, "Sorry buddy. And yes, I already knew"

"So why didn't you tell me earlier that she is already engaged?" He said in an irritated tone.

"Dude, I was just enjoying the state you were in." Akash grinned, "I wanted her to tell you so that you would have no doubts. Hope she wasn't too rash on you; Was she?"

Prakhar got off the bed, grinding his teeth, while leaving the room, he grumbled lines from another Hindi film song, *"Dil mera tod diya usney, buraa kyun maanu... (She broke my heart, why should I feel bad though...)"* and sprinting down the stairs he added, "My turn too will also come, son, stay safe."

Akash unable to stop his laughter, clapped his hands and replied, "Bro, don't get so angry. See you at office tomorrow." and then the firing of Prakhar's motorcycle could be heard receding.

With a little mischief, a little fun and a little bullying, life can be saved from being boring. While living alone, Akash would occasionally pull out such little chances of having fun.

It was eleven o'clock. He picked up all books that were scattered across the bed and placed them on the shelf. Sliding the phone in his pocket, he left the room, crossed the road, and entered the cyber cafe. Sitting in front of a computer, he went through the unread e-mails. No sign of reply from HR. He felt that maybe something went amiss in the interview. He closed the mailbox, picked up the phone and started looking for something in it.

Yesterday's chat had kept coming back to his mind throughout everything he had done till now. He opened the chatting application and started checking if there are any pending messages from yesterday's User Id. When he was convinced that she was not online, he turned off the computer and left the cafe.

Since Prakhar's broken heart episode had left no time for breakfast, Akash's stomach was growling ferociously with hunger. After pacifying his stomach in a nearby restaurant, he came back to his room.

He had to finish reading his ongoing book, and return it to the library before evening, so he started swimming through the currents of words in the last few pages.

The month of June had begun. The monsoon season was on its verge of beginning. Sometimes in the evening, a few raindrops would sprinkle the ground. The city was waiting for the weather to switch sides. The days between the departing summer and the arriving monsoons, are usually prone to their own distinct mood swings. The nights would become partially humid and partially dry, the mornings smelled wet, and the day would feel tangled. The vigor of passing breezes would ease the mind and gave signs of the onset of pleasant drizzles.

The clock stroke nine. Akash got ready, left his room, and proceeded towards the bus stop. After a while the bus arrived, and he hopped onboard. Half an hour later, he got down at the bus stop in front of his office. The first thing he did after reaching his cubicle was a quick glance through his office e-mails. He realized that his day wasn't going to be demanding today.

Getting up from his seat, he peeped into the opposite cubicle, and discovered that Prakhar had not reached yet. Recalling yesterday's fierce farewell, he muttered with a smile, "Looks like Romeo may not come today" and then began doing his pending work.

It was twelve o'clock and he was still staring at the computer screen. Having worked continuously for a couple of hours, he thought of taking a break. So, he brought a cup of coffee from the coffee machine and sat back comfortably in his seat. While sipping coffee, the words from that chat window kept popping in his mind, which brought a slight smile to his lips.

Soon it would be lunch time, so he opened the chatting application on his computer and saw an unread message from Avni was waiting for him. The timestamp was from just a few minutes back -

"Hi Akash, hope you are doing good"

She was online at that time. So, Akash replied -

"Yes, I am fine" and he looked intently at the screen and waited for her next message.

For quite some time there was no message from her end. Akash kept staring at the screen. As some more time passed and he realized that Avni wasn't typing anything, his discomfort grew. Even though he was aware that she was still a stranger, a little restlessness had begun in his mind, and it clearly reflected on his face.

When no message came for a long time, he decided to take the conversation ahead and typed -

"How are you?"

But before sending the message, he held his finger in the air playing with his own hesitation that was holding him back. Perhaps an old habit, which had dominated him until now, prevented him from talking openly with a stranger.

He put his hand back on the table and sat there for a while. Then, on second thoughts, he deleted the message he had typed and covered his eyes with his palms as if he was feeling regret about something.

After a few minutes, when he opened his eyes, Avni's reply was waiting for him on the screen -

"Hello ji"

Akash felt as if Avni was sitting so far away but had understood his hesitation -

"Hello Avni" Akash replied.

"What's up?" Avni typed.

Akash was a bit comfortable now and he also completed the formality and typed –

"All good… You tell me."

"Am good too. I am in college now."

"Ok. I am also in office."

"Ok. By the way, what sort of work are you into?"

"I write programs… I mean, I work with an IT company."

"Oh! so, you have done your engineering?"

"Yeah, and you?"

"I have done my M.Sc."

"Ok. That's good"

"Well, what's so good about it?"

"I also wanted to complete Masters, but could not do it"

"Hey! Why is that so?"

                                          Rendezvous

"That's a strange tale, leave it. Are you from Nainital?"

"Oh no, I am from Delhi. My parents are there, I came here for my job posting."

"Wow! You have set a new trend"

"What trend?"

"People go to metropolitan cities from small towns in search of jobs, and you have left Delhi for Nainital."

":) :) I desperately wanted to get out of crowded Delhi and luckily got a job here."

"Well, small towns have their own charms. There must be no dearth of peaceful moments."

"Yes, in a way, life is a much easier. There's no rush about anything and the weather is always nice."

"Enough, don't make me jealous."

"Ha... at least one of your weaknesses has been uncovered."

"What weakness?"

"I found a way to make you feel jealous."

"Oho... Ok... You've got some sharp brains there."

"You cannot beat a gold medalist."

"Wow! And then there are people like me who somehow pass exams.:)"

"Let it be... Now you are making it up."

"No... Really. It's my good luck that I even passed. By the way, I also got to know one of your weaknesses."

"And what's that?"

"That it's easy to fool you."

":-) :-) :-) :-)"

":) :) : :) :)"

This kind of an interaction was a new experience for both Akash and Avni. On one end was Akash - ever engrossed in himself, and not so easy to be understood. However, he was surprising himself. Accustomed to speaking in few words, he was surprising himself by the ease with which he could get carried away with flow of words. On the other end, Avni too found herself flying like a free bird - chirping and singing.

The sky was being covered by dark clouds, as if they wanted to come closer and hold earth in their embrace.

Their conversation kept flowing freely - Tales, stories, poems, likes-dislikes kept getting exchanged from both sides. Then, just as one wakes up from a state of hypnosis and returns to the real world, Akash came out of this zone, when he saw that his watch was showing half past one.

"Hey, listen, my lunch break is almost over. Later I have a scheduled meeting.

"Oh! I had lost the sense of time. My lecture too with begin from 2 o'clock. Go on then, you go for your lunch."

"Okay then, take care."

"You too, bye."

"Bye"

While chatting, Akash felt as if there was something else that he wanted to write about but couldn't figure out why he couldn't. Since it was already late for lunch, he rushed to the office canteen and after gobbling down whatever he could within 5 mins and ran towards the meeting room.

His next two or three days were too hectic for him to do anything else other than work. He would reach his room late at night and then leave for office early in the morning. In this hustle and bustle, his chat with Avni had been put on an abrupt pause. Nevertheless, even in the short breaks he took, all that occupied his mind was the work that he had just completed and was about to do. Even while being trapped in such workload, sometimes a light feather of memory would tickle his thoughts and he would spontaneously smile. In those moments, he would leave work in the middle, recline in his chair by resting his neck on his palms, close his eyes, and would let his mind wander for a few minutes and then got back to work.

Completion wasn't visible anywhere on the horizon of his work schedule. It went on growing akin to the tail of the mighty Hanuman. When Akash returned to his room at night, it was already eleven o'clock. He was fatigued due to continuous work over the last few days. As soon as he entered the room, he let his body collapse in the softness of his bed. He kept staring at the ceiling fan, then got up, changed his clothes, and went back to bed. Somehow, the tiredness of his limbs and mind didn't bring sleep to his eyes. For a while, he kept tossing and turning around in bed. His mind was running simultaneously in multiple lanes of thoughts. Soon sleep took him in its embrace as his thoughts floated and turned into dreams.

Early next morning, he woke up with his eyes taking comfort in the dark sky outside the window. His alarm clock was ringing five. He came out of the room and went up the stairs to his terrace.

The stars twinkling in the sky beneath the thin sheet of moon light, a slightly cool breeze caressing the silence of the morning, made the sky feel fresher than it had ever felt. This made him wonder about the number of mornings he had spent in midst of such beauty. But today it felt new in a different way.

Sometimes life presents new lanes, and we set out on them out of a spontaneous urge, without giving a second thought to where those lanes will take us. Akash was also eager to set out on one of such paths, perhaps without any concerns about the destination.

The stars were slowly dissolving as the sky took on new colors originating from the vermilion that the horizon was brimming with. The birds were busy singing different songs, but in unison. Akash took a deep breath and then went back to his room.

Gearing up for the weekend, Akash decided to spend his Saturday in the library. He had to return the previous book and borrow a new one complying with his personal literary culture of completing a book per week.

After having breakfast, he reached the library at ten o'clock and started browsing through books. He read the initial couple of pages of every book and if the prose clicked with him, he pressed it to his chest, then go ahead in search of the next book. Thus, collecting four or five books of his choice, he settled down at a nearby table, bowed his head and disappeared into the world of words.

At exactly twelve o'clock, ding-dong from a pendulum clock hanging on the wall of the library hall, distracted him. He raised his head and looked around the hall, then closed the books and reached the reception. Taking one book, he left the rest, and left the library. He slowed down as he passed by the cyber cafe in front of his PG. Before he could make up his mind, his feet took eager steps towards the doorway. He opened the chatting application and saw two messages from Avni were waiting for him. First one had been sent 3 days ago and the second one had arrived last afternoon. Both the messages had nothing other than, "Hello Akash".

He replied, "Hi Avni, how are you?" And logged off after sending the message. When he returned to his room, he got engrossed in the new book for a while, but today his mind was wandering away from the pages. He was unable to understand why a strange restlessness was gripping him today. Prakhar was also out of town and Akash didn't have any urge to go anywhere. To get rid of this inner unrest, he went out and stood in the balcony, from where he watched the people coming and going. His eyes rested on the cybercafe and without giving it a second thought, he walked down, entered the café, logged in to a computer and then the chatting application. He saw that Avni was online, but there was no reply to his message.

After waiting for a while, Akash sent - "Hello Avni"

Avni's prompt reply came "Hi Akash. Is everything ok?"

"Yes! And you?"

"I'm fine."

"I mean, are you fine from health perspective?"

"Yes, nothing is wrong with my health."

"Ok."

For some time, both sat silently in two far away towns, in front of their computers, without exchanging any messages. Then thinking something, Akash typed - "Something strange is happening in my mind today."

"Okay, is there a problem?"

"No."

"Perhaps the story of the book I was reading might have had an effect."

"Oh! You were reading a novel?"

"Yes."

"O Yes! You had mentioned that you love to read. Which book is it?"

"KASAP. Manohar Shyam Joshi's novel."

"I am not fond of reading at all. Academic books occupy all my time."

"My spare time is spent only in reading."

"I wonder how people read such thick novels."

"It's not about the pages. How the story is told, is what matters. That keeps driving the reader's interest."

"Well, how many books do you read?"

"One per week, for sure."

"Ok! I read poems occasionally."

"Hmm..."

When there was no further message from Avni, Akash again wrote to her -

"You there or lost somewhere?"

"Hey, I am here. Just that someone was calling me."

"Good."

"Listen, I need to rush to the staff room. Will you be online now?"

"Okay, Will it take long?"

"No, I will be back in just a few minutes."

Akash saw the clock which was about to begin the next hour. He was also feeling extremely hungry. But more than hunger his veins were filled with restlessness due to Avni's elongated absence. He was busy trying to make sense of this restlessness when the reply came on the screen -

"I'm back."

And Akash's restlessness came to a sharp halt.

He typed - "You took so long!"

"Oho! It's been only a few minutes."

"And I was waiting on an empty stomach here."

"Oh, sorry you haven't had lunch yet."

"No."

"Then go and have lunch. We can talk tomorrow."

Akash didn't reply. He felt that their conversation should keep flowing for a some more time. Then Avni's next message came, "Didn't leave for lunch yet?"

"Need to go. But okay, I'll go a bit late."

"Oho! No, you don't need to go late! I don't feel good about you staying hungry."

"It's OK."

"Not okay at all, get up now."

"But I had something else to talk about."

"Oh, it's okay, isn't it? We can continue talking tomorrow."

"Maybe I'll be busy tomorrow. There are some other plans.

"Alright. Tell me then. What did you want to talk about?"

"No, nothing specific that way."

"Sure?"

"Yeah"

"Okay then you go have your lunch."

"Ok, you take care."

"You too..."

Akash stood up and was about to log off, when Avni's message came on the screen

"Listen…"

"Yeah, what happened?"

"Tomorrow I'm not free either. Next week is going to be tough."

"So, you won't be able to log in?"

"Most probably."

Akash, who was quite at ease till now, suddenly felt the fear of missing out on something important. The lines on his forehead grew darker and he sat in the chair again. There was no further message from Avni as well. Perhaps, both were hesitating to ask anything. For a while he just kept running his fingers on the keyboard, then deleted what he had typed. In the meantime, Avni's reply came,

"I will message you. Then we can decide the time."

"On the phone?"

"Yes. Can you give me your number?"

Akash's heartbeats suddenly spiked up. Never had an unknown girl asked him for his phone number. In a dilemma, he was wondering what could be the harm in sharing his number? Maybe she is asking just as a friend, so that it is easier to coordinate. However, it may also be that she wants to test if he is that kind of a man who easily shares his phone number with any woman!

Since the pause on Akash's end went on for a bit too long, Avni wrote -

"It's ok if you don't want to give your number. I had asked just like that."

"Oh no, nothing like that.", followed by which Akash typed his number.

"Thanks! I'll message you then."

"Ok now let me go for lunch."

":) Yes! Sure, bye, take care."

" :) Bye."

Akash was in a strange mood after leaving the cybercafe. It was as if he had sleepwalked through having lunch and reaching his room. Lying in bed for a long time, who knows what thoughts he kept diving into.

During his last conversation with Avni, something had changed between them. But Akash couldn't determine what exactly had changed. The question kept troubling him like a complex knot that forms on bunch of threads. He spent his day trying to ease this knot.

It wasn't like any other Sunday morning. As far as he could see, the sky was filled with a mellow light. There was a distinctive fragrance in the air that was filling up his being.

He spent the whole day in his room. Neither did he read much, nor did he go anywhere outside. Whenever he felt hungry, he simply cooked something in the room.

It was evening and he was ironing his office clothes to wear on the next day. That's when the phone buzzed. Assuming it to be some spam message, he ignored it. Finishing all his domestic work, he left the room, as he was feeling suffocated due to his self-imposed lock-in for the whole day. He wandered around in the park for a long time and then went out and ate and drank something in a nearby restaurant, after which he returned to his room.

As was his habit, whenever he had to go somewhere not too far from his room, he would leave his phone in the room itself. As soon as he entered, he picked up the phone. He saw notifications of two unread messages from an unknown number. Thinking they are promotional messages, he thought of deleting it, but instead he opened it,

"Is it possible to talk? - Avni."
Then he read the second message which had arrived a while back.
"Message me if you're free. -Avni."
Akash saved the number then he replied -
"Hello Avni."
After some time, Avni replied.
"Hi."
Akash typed -
"You wanted to talk about something?"
"No, nothing special."
"Ok, did you have your dinner?"
"Yes, and you?"
"Mine's done too."

Avni did not message any further. After waiting for some time, Akash kept the phone aside and picked up his book.

As he went with the flow of the novel, he didn't realize when the clock stuck 10:00 PM. Akash kept the book aside and turned off the light. Sleep seemed to be far away from him, and his mind kept going back to Avni's message – "Is it possible to talk?"

What did she have on her mind? She didn't tell even after he had asked. Maybe she had written it just like that! Or maybe it was her way to share her phone number! Such questions kept his mind busy for a while.

Next day at office was just like any other weekday. Akash was working in his own flow, when Prakhar patted him on his shoulder using a little extra force than he normally would, "So bro, how has life been treating you?"

Akash who was flying through clouds of thoughts came crashing down to the ground.

                                        Rendezvous

"Easy man, easy!"

"Oh! You didn't get hurt; Did you?"

"No dude! Men don't feel pain." And both laughed.

"How was your trip to Poona?"

"Debacle, dude. I couldn't find a single prospective customer."

"So, you have no lambs to butcher this time?" Akash laughed.

"No man, the product has no strengths."

"Then pass on the feedback to the management."

"Already submitted, but nothing is going to happen."

"You are so brimming with negativity, man!"

"That's exactly why I spend time with you." Grinning, Prakhar continued, "You are positive, I am negative. That neutralizes us."

And both burst out laughing.

At night, Akash reached his room late than usual, changed his clothes and went straight to bed. It was the first week of July and the rainy season was now in full swing. It rained intermittently throughout the day. It was still drizzling while Akash was sitting in the darkness of his room. When lightning crackled up the sky, his whole room was drenched with light for a moment. He relished the rhythmic sound of raindrops. The window was open, so a gust of wind was bringing in light showers, sprinkling the room intermittently. Akash turned on the radio on his mobile, put his headphones on his ears and snuggled the pillows in the bed. Radio FM was filling him up with a song that went well with the weather -

aaj maine dil se, baadalon se milke

sapnon ki baarish se kaliyaan sajaa ke

beheki umangon se khushboo churaa ke

halki si boondon mein, leheron ki goonjon mein

goom ho jaana re, doob jaana re

mujhko doob jaane re, tere paas aana re

While listening to the song, he was reading the messages from last night which were exchanged between him and Avni. After reading, he casually sent a message to Avni -

'Hi how are you?'

Then he felt he shouldn't have messaged her so late at 10:30 PM. She might have slept. So, he turned off the radio and kept the mobile aside. Just a few minutes later his phone buzzed, and he saw Avni's message -

'I am fine. You didn't sleep yet?'

'I was just going to sleep. Isn't it way past your bedtime?'

'Yes! I have come to Delhi. Mother is not well.

'Oh! What happened?'

'She has a fever. So, papa had called me."

'Oh, ok'

Akash did not send any further message. Somehow, he felt that he should talk to Avni. He thought that if he is asking about his condition by messaging, then she might not mind talking. Hesitatingly he messaged - 'Can I call you?'

Avni replied -

'Now?'

'Only if it wouldn't be a problem for you.'

'Yes! You can.'

'Okay, I am calling.'

Akash was now confused how to start the conversation? What was he going to say? What if he asked about her mother? Or should he say something else? He was still thinking when Avni's name flashed on his phone screen -

Akash picked up and said softly -

"Hello…"

"Hi! Akash."

"Hi! Avni."

"Do you stay up late every day?"

  Rendezvous

"No, I came late from office today. Otherwise, I have a habit of going to bed early at night and waking up early in the morning.

"Oh well I stay up till late. I don't like waking up early."

"You may not have heard the phrase 'Early to bed early to rise'; Have you?"

Avni giggled and said, "I know, I know… But I have no intention of implementing such things."

"Being a teacher, what kind of habits are you passing on to your students!" Akash quipped.

Avni said sarcastically, "Right… I teach at college, not at kindergarten."

"Ok… How is your mother's health now?"

"She is better now. She had got a viral infection. It may take three to four days to recover."

"Okay, then nothing serious."

"Na… Not at all."

"By the way, who all are at home?"

"Mom, dad, and my younger brother. He goes to college. What about your family?" Avni asked.

"Mom, dad and a younger sister. She is perceiving her master's degree at present. Dad is a Central government employee." Said Akash in a single breath.

"So, do you go home frequently or not much?"

"I go only for Diwali or during year-end closing."

"You live alone; Don't you?"

"Yes, I have rented a room in a PG."

"Then what do you do about your daily food? Do you cook on your own?"

"No, I eat outside."

"So, you never learnt how to cook!" Avni jokingly asked.

"A little bit, like poha, chai sometimes Maggi…."

"Ha ha ha… that's not what you can claim as cooking skills." Avni said in a bubbly voice.

"Yes-yes! I know." Akash shrugged and replied, "Well, you are speaking as if you are a top chef."

"Don't even try to underestimate me. If you taste my food, you will keep licking your fingers for a couple of days." Avni said proudly

"In that case, I will have to visit you for grand dinner soon."

"Sure, why not?" Avni said with a laugh. "By the way, I thought that you are a serious type of a person, but you are not all that serious."

"And I thought that you would be that teacher type – *khadoos (strict, stubborn, snobbish)*" Akash had now completely opened-up due to this round of teasing and counter-teasing.

"O ho! Let it be. You won't understand what value a teacher like me holds for college students." said Avni with a chuckle.

You are right. They wouldn't have possibly met anyone as *khadoos* as you." Akash teased her,

"Whatever… I know, I am the favorite of my students. That's what matters." Avni said proudly

"Ok, fine… I surrender." Akash said with a chuckle.

"This is the eternal truth, child. So, you have no way other than to believe it." Avni giggled.

"Fine, you won…" Akash said.

"It's quite late. Aren't you feeling sleepy?"

Akash felt like telling her that he was feeling good to talk to her at this time. Even if he goes late to bed one day, it will not matter.

"Hey, have you already slept?" Avni said with a chuckle from that side.

"Hey! No - no." Akash said shuddering out of his thought.

"I can understand as you need to go to office in the morning." Avni said,

"Yes! I have to leave at nine in the morning."

"Then go to sleep now or else you will be late tomorrow and then you will curse me." advised Avni

"Arrey! Why will I curse you? And I won't be late. Don't worry." Akash said.

　　　　　　　　　　　　　　　Rendezvous

"Ok, tell me something. Why do you live alone? I mean, you can easily share a flat with a friend; right?"

"I used to live in a shared flat, but then I realized that it's better to stay alone."

"Oh! Did you end up in a quarrel or something?"

"Oh no! It simply didn't work out, so I took a separate room."

"So, you prefer living on your own."

"Yes, maybe."

"Hmm… I am incapable of living alone."

"Why? Do you feel scared? Like, what if a ghost crawls up to your bed at night?" Akash said with a scary voice.

"Oh! Now don't scare me." Avni said softly,

"So, you do feel scared." Akash laughed.

"Everyone feels scared at some point or the other. As if you are too macho to feel scared." Avni said in an irritated tone.

Akash understood that she was a bit annoyed, "Listen, I was just pulling your leg."

"Hmm" Avni said softly and then continued, "It's too late, let's call it a night."

"Avni, are you feeling angry at me due to the whole scaring thing?" Akash asked

"No, I am not. I am just saying so that you don't miss out on your sleep tonight."

"Oh ok. I thought that's why you didn't like my joking around with you."

"Oh, you think too much." Avni said innocently.

"Ok then, good night" Akash said

"Good night." Avni said softly and disconnected.

Akash kept the phone aside and closed his eyes as he turned over to his left side. Avni's sweet, melodious voice was still echoing softly in his ears. Still under the intoxication of Avni's voice, he heard his phone vibrate - Avni's message flashed on his screen - "Sweet Dreams".

Akash's smile wouldn't cease as he stared at the bright light of the phone and closed his eyes gliding into his journey of sleep guided by the echoes of Avni's voice.

Next day, no call or message was exchanged between them. Akash thought that Avni must have her hands full, taking care of her mother. However, when he came back to his room at night, he thought that he should check on Avni over a message. He messaged, then spread his legs on the bed, rested his back on the wall, and peered out of the window. A light breeze was bringing in petrichor. Akash thought it must be raining somewhere nearby. He closed his eyes and inhaled deeply, as if he intended to fill himself up with fragrance.

He dialed the phone number of his home. His mother answered. After asking about the well-being of his mother and father, many other topics came up. Papa asked whether he will be able to visit home for Diwali holidays. This year their Diwali plans included a family outing, so they discussed about preparations for the trip.

Disconnecting the phone, he got up from bed and stood outside in the balcony, looking over the crowded road below. After a while, the noise got too much for him to bear, so he came back to his room. When he looked at the phone, Avni's missed call was visible on the screen. He had not heard the ring because of the noise outside. He called Avni -

Avni picked up, "Hi"

"Hello" Akash said softly "Sorry I didn't hear the ring. I was outside in the balcony."

"No problem, I saw your message and called."

"Well, how is your mother's health now?"

"Oh man, her fever is showing no signs of reducing. I am losing my mind seeing her this way." Avni said in a voice brimming with anxiety.

"Viral fever takes some time to recede, and there's age factor as well. So, you may need to stay patient through this phase." Akash said calmly.

"Yes, maybe you are right, but I am very close to my mother that's why I get easily tense when I see her suffering."

"She'll be fine in a day or two, don't worry."

"Hmmmm..."

"You know, you say 'Hmmmm...' like kids do."

                                              Rendezvous

Avni giggled a little shyly, "Thanks."

"Thanks for what?"

"For pepping me up. You made me smile in an instant. I have spent the whole day worrying."

"Shukriya, Shukriya."

"Wow! You speak Urdu too?"

"Not really. It's just that my reading habit has added a few words to my vocab."

"That's nice."

"You know 'Shukriya' is also a female name in Arabic. Which means thankful and there's also a male name 'Shukri' with the same meaning."

"Where did you read that?"

"Just somewhere… I can't recollect the source."

"What kind of books do you read?"

"I am into reading Hindi literature and sometimes English novels."

"Wow! And do you read poetry too?"

"Yeah, sometimes that too."

"Then I am sure, you must be writing too; Don't you?"

"No-no, not at all."

"Akash ji, come-on, don't lie." said Avni nudging him to open-up, "Go ahead, recite something."

Akash could not refuse her, "Well wait, let me bring my diary."

"Okay, come quickly." Avni said with a smile.

Akash pulled out an old leather-bound diary from his bag and sat down on the bed. He turned the pages to find a good poem. He had not written anything new for a while, so he prepared himself to recite an old poem.

"Hello! Are you still there on the phone?" He asked Avni.

"What else? I am waiting for you." she said impatiently, "You are going to recite something; Aren't you?"

"Yeah, yeah, wait, Are you always in such a hurry for everything?"

"Yeah, you may be right about that." Avni said in an effervescent voice, "Now please proceed with the recital, Sire."

"Okay, then listen" and Akash began reciting some of his lines.

"woh fakir

niklaa phir meri gali se

gungunaatey huye, muskuraate huye

jeewan ka nichod chehre pe odhey huye

samjhaane ko wahin do chaar sabak

zindagaani, vafaa, pyaar aur dard."

"that fakir

strolls through my lane

humming, smiling,

the mist of life playing on his face,

singing of the same four lessons

life, loyalty, love, and pain"

"Well done, bravo." Avni chirped, "But it is serious." She said keeping her opinion brief.

Akash smiled and said, "Yeah, I had written it just like that. Maybe I was in philosophical mood at that point."

"Haven't you written any romantic poem?" Avni asked, her voice dancing in Akash's ear.

"I used to write those type of poems during my college days." Akash said quivering.

"Aha! Then what are you waiting for? Go on, recite one of those." Avni said chirpily.

"No, leave those poems aside. They were not that good." Akash said.

"No, forget about escaping from this moment and recite something romantic." Avni said in an assertive voice.

"Ok-ok, give me a few minutes. I will have to search for those." Akash said while turning the pages.

Then he recited some lines from one of his old poems.

"Listen then..."

"teri mast nigaahon mein doob jaana hain mujhe

yun iss qadar tujhmein samaa jaanaa hain mujhe

phir na bichadenge, kho gaya hoon iss qadar

paas aao ke behek jaana hain mujhe"

a desire to drown in your playful gaze,

a desire to merge with you in such ways

that leaves us ever inseparable,

in you i have lost my self thus,

come closer, i want to wander deeper in you

"Oh my God" Avni exclaimed, "Dude, you write so well!" Avni clapping from there said.

"Thanks" Akash said expressing his gratitude.

"Now tell me who was the girl you wrote this for?" Avni asked teasingly.

"There was no one." Akash said shyly as his fingers brushed through his hair.

"You want me to believe there was no one to inspire such a passionate poem? You take me for a fool? Come-on, tell me." Avni was now adamant.

"No yaar, there was seriously no girl." Akash said trying to dodge the question.

"If you don't want to tell me, it's fine." Avni said calmly. "It just means that you don't consider me your friend."

Akash's tone grew defensive, "How do I make you understand that there was really no girl?"

"Ok, I will believe you, but for that you will have to recite another romantic poem." Avni ordered,

"That's all for today." replied Akash

"Ok, then I guess my intuition was right; Wasn't it? Avni asked.

"What intuition?" Akash asked.

"That you don't think of me as a friend?" Avni asked

Akash was silent for a while then said slowly, "But I do think of you like a friend.

"Like a friend! Hmmm…" Avni exclaimed in a thoughtful tone.

Akash felt that Avni didn't like the skepticism in his voice. So, he clarified, "Arrey, I meant, of-course you are my friend."

"Sealed deal, then?" Avni asked with a laugh.

Akash also laughed out realizing that she had been just pulling his leg.

As the days passed by, the hesitation between them mellowed down and gradually they opened-up increasingly more with each conversation. Soon both found themselves spending time, casually talking, joking, laughing, and sharing anecdotes every day without having to think before talking. Sometimes they would explain things to each other, sometimes tease each other, sometimes get angry and at other times make peace after a disagreement. Both were riding waves of a new ocean of excitement. Roads for a new journey could be seen sprouting up between two people who were strangers just a few weeks ago.

***

His face had developed a glow of a different shade and an unmistakable aura could be felt emanating from him, while he kept wondering about this new path life was taking him on. What kind of events are these? Whose voice keeps singing in my ears? Why are my heartbeats not in my control? Why does everything feel a little different, even though everything around me is the same as it was?

The changes were clearly visible in Akash's behavior. A person who once spent days and nights with his head buried in pages of books, now lived more in the world of daydreams. The pleasant smile had established its own tent on his lips. Flowers in bloom seemed more beautiful to him than before. Winds seemed to carry a sweet chirping voice especially for him. He had found a special rhythm in the raindrops. Probably love was slowly sprouting in his heart.

The monsoon season had reached its final phase. Every evening, Akash had developed a habit of sitting in a nearby park. Breathing in the fragrance of flowers and watching the leaves moving on branches of trees, enabled him to feel Avni's presence around him. One such evening when he was sitting in the park after returning from his office, he received a call from Avni.

Usually, they used to talk at night, and would exchange messages during the rest of the day. In such a situation, seeing Avni's call at this time of the evening, a sense of apprehension grew in his mind. It is natural to feel anxious when there is a break in pattern when you associate someone with certain hours and activities. Either it comes as a pleasant surprise or raises a flag for concern.

Akash answered the call without greeting 'Hi' or 'Hello' and asked directly, "Are you alright?"

"Whoa! No greetings, no salutations, you are firing straight questions today!" asked Avni.

"Ah! Just that you never call at this hour, that's why I feared something was wrong."

"Akash, you're too much. I don't call you during this time because you are busy, and I also don't get free until 8 o'clock." Avni explained.

"Ok, got it, but you're fine, aren't you?" Akash asked again.

"I am completely fine, and I have taken a leave tomorrow." Avni said happily.

"Oh wow! Well, what occasion calls for a holiday tomorrow?"

"Just like that! I thought it would be nice of me to call and harass you throughout the day." Avni replied with a laugh.

"Okay, so that's the plan! Now that I know, I am not going to pick up the phone tomorrow." Akash said with a chuckle.

"Don't pick up. I will keep on calling even then." Avni spoke in a mischievous voice.

"So, do you mean, tomorrow is going to be my last day in office?" Akash said while exhaling.

"Oh, why are you saying that?" Avni asked.

"Madame, if you call all day long, then where will I find time to work? Then no-one will give me money for being on personal calls. They will tell me to stay at home and speak on the phone as much as I want, and that someone else would be more than happy to take care of all the work that's assigned to me. Namaskar." Changing his voice, Akash said dramatically.

His tone triggered peals of laughter in Avni. Saving her breath, controlling her laughter, she said, "You will definitely give me a stomachache." She was still laughing.

After a while, when her laughter ceased, she further said, "Akash you are very talented."

"Yes, I know." Akash replied by raising his eyebrows and nodding his head.

"See, a little praise and our sir changes colors." Avni said with a chuckle.

Akash laughed and said, "And you are no less."

"Yes! I know." Avni said, imitating Akash's voice and then giggled again.

Akash laughed softly again then said "Okay listen now I will go back to my room. It's closing time at the park."

"All right. I'll call at night." Avni said.

"Now we have already talked so much. Why don't you call tomorrow? After all, you have taken a leave just to call me; right?" Akash said in a teasing tone.

"No, you are not allowed to cheat on our night calls." Avni said loudly, then after a deliberate pause, "Well, just for two minutes then."

"Okay Baba but only for two minutes," Akash said, then Avni replied in a hurry. "Ok sir."

Akash had his dinner early that night and then went straight to the room. There was a strange restlessness within him. He kept checking his phone repeatedly. It was clear from the tautness of his cheeks that he was waiting for Avni's call.

The clock had struck ten and there was no sign of Avni's call. Akash was leaning by the window, watching people passing by. Then a message appeared on the phone. Avni had written that she would call in a while.

Akash took the phone in his hand and sat down on the bed stretching his legs. His thumb kept caressing the phone screen, as if it were something precious, while Avni's voice was playing in his mind.

The phone rang. Avni's name appeared, and he hurriedly answered the call." "Hello Avni."

"Hello ji" Avni replied softly.

"Why are you talking with such whispers?"

"Uff! I'm just tired."

"Had you gone out somewhere?"

"Yeah, staff's dinner plan got made all of a sudden."

"Ok, then you must have had a lot of fun." Akash asked cheerfully.

"The food was great, but I wasn't able to enjoy my time there." Avni said with regret in her voice.

"Why?"

"Don't know."

"Are you feeling well?" Akash asked with concern in his voice.

"Yes, Akash. I'm perfectly fit and I even danced quite a lot there. Avni said chirpily. Akash could hear bangles in the background.

"Hmm, looks like you got groomed-up quite a bit for the party. I can hear your bangles." Akash said.

"Yes, I have bangles in both wrists, and you know, I am wearing a pink colored sari, with a lustrous border." There was something different in Avni's voice today.

"Oho! I am sure, some people must have gone home with their hearts in their mouths." Akash said in a merry voice.

"Yeah, what else." Avni replied in a note of faux pride in her voice.

Then paused for a while and said, "Akash you know, I was told by my colleague that my face has been glowing since a few days. I didn't know that."

"Ok! I think, she must be lying." Akash said teasingly.

"Whatever! You haven't even seen me; How can you say that? Avni said in an irritated tone.

In that instant, Akash wondered, how would it have been if Avni was in front of him? He was still immersed in thoughts when some voices emerged on the phone from Avni's side. The sound of bangles in Avni's hands was melting in his ears. Avni asked softly, "Hello Akash, are you still there?"

"Yes, I am here." Akash said.

"I don't know where you get lost in between. Don't do this when you are talking to me, do you understand? Avni said scolding him.

"As you wish, my lord." Akash replied, slightly bowing his head.

The tone of Akash's voice made Avni laugh. Akash was relishing the sound of her laughter.

"Hey, listen, I want to change into something comfortable now. Will you wait for me?" Avni asked.

"I have to go to office tomorrow. If I don't sleep, how am I supposed to work?" Akash asked.

"Oh yes! Well then, we will talk tomorrow." said Avni.

"Yeah, ok! You also take rest now. You must be tired."

"Talking to you has made all my fatigue go away." Avni replied and then fell silent.

Akash also remained silent for a few moments then said, "Good night."

"Good night, Akash." There was a gentle innocence in Avni's voice.

Outside the window, the night felt as if it was in the best phase of its youth. The cool breeze flowing through the window had filled the room with a distinct fragrance. The moon was peeping through the skylight window. Its light was bathing Akash's face, and somewhere far away, the voice of a Chakor was echoing.

The next day, work kept Akash occupied in his office. In the evening, when he was returning home riding pillion on Prakhar's bike, a car hit them from behind near the signal. Prakhar lost his balance and fall on the sidewalk. Since the motorcycle was at a low speed, Prakhar suffered minor injuries on his hands. Akash's leg had got trapped under the bike, and he was unable to get up. People helped him sit up. As his leg was not visible, Akash could see a long cut in his leg and the lower part of his trousers was drenched in blood.

Somehow with the help of people, he reached a nearby hospital. There the doctors checked and observed that the cut was deep but there was no injury to the bone. He returned to his room after taking some instructions and medicines. Prakhar had called a friend to help him support Akash till his room.

The pain was severe, and his leg was bandaged downwards from his knee. This left him immobile. After taking medicines, sleep took over his tired body.

He woke up by the ringing of his phone. With great difficulty he opened his eyes. His body was hot with fever, maybe due to the immense pain in his leg. He had left his phone on the table while entering the room. Somehow, he got up and limped to the table. By then the ringing had died down. He picked up the phone and saw it was half past ten in the night. There were four calls from Avni. He called Avni -

"Hello Akash." Avni immediately picked up the phone as she was eagerly waiting for that call.

"Hello." Akash said softly. The pain was clearly visible in his voice.

"Where were you and why do you sound that way?" the concern in Avni's voice grew with each word.

"Uh… I was sleeping." Akash said slowly.

"Did you fall asleep? You went to sleep early today? You are unwell; Aren't you?" the concern in Avni's voice persisted.

"Nothing has happened. I'm fine Avni." This time the pain in the voice was clearer.

"I cannot believe that. You voice doesn't seem to support your words. You are not well for sure. Why are you hiding things from me? What happened? Please tell me." Avni's voice was now a little nervous.

Akash understood that Avni's doubts were inescapable, and she would keep asking until he told her.

"There was a bike accident this evening. There is a cut in my leg and it's hurting a lot I did hear your previous call, but it got disconnected before I could reach the phone." Akash told her all at once.

"Oh my God." That's all Avni could say Then after a pause, she asked, "Akash, is the pain unbearable?" There was a caress in her voice.

"Yes! It is as of now. There is also a slight fever. But I'll be fine in a day or two, don't you worry." Akash said trying to comfort her.

"I don't know how much you are injured. But I know you are in a lot of pain. Akash how will you take care of yourself? Is there anyone who can take care of you?" Avni's voice had changed somewhat.

"Yes! There are a couple of friends living here. Food will come from their house, and I am taking my medicines."

"That's fine, Akash. But you will have trouble walking too. So, who will take care of you in the room? You live there alone, don't you?"

"Avni, you are worrying unnecessarily."

"I don't know. You must recover as soon as possible." There was a bit of heaviness in Avni's voice

"Ok, I will take care of myself. Listen, I am feeling uncontrollably sleepy. Maybe it's the effect of my medicines."

"Okay you rest and ensure that you take someone's help. Don't start doing everything by yourself." the same heaviness constant in her voice.

"Sure, I will. Listen, Good night and bye for now."

"Please take care, Akash." And Avni disconnected the phone.

Akash woke up early next morning and slowly sat up in bed. When he looked at his leg, he could see swelling in the lower part. He raised his feet and as soon as he placed them on the ground, he yelled with pain, then hurriedly sat back on his bed. For a while he just sat there thinking about something. Then somehow, he got up and went to the bathroom. After returning he lay down again. His head was feeling heavier. He closed his eyes and stayed lying on his back

His phone began ringing besides him. He saw it was Prakhar's. The two talked for some time. Prakhar told that he is better now. He said he will send tiffin for Akash with a man today, which will have breakfast and lunch. In the evening he will give another tiffin, and, in the morning, he will take it back. He also told Akash that he had given the news in the office last night, so there is no need to call separately.

Akash got up, leaned against the wall, and picking up the diary kept nearby, he started writing something in it. He couldn't write for long because his head had begun to feel heavier now. He closed his eyes and rested his head on the wall. He had remained sitting this way for a while

                                                    Rendezvous

when the phone rang. Without opening his eyes, he answered the call -

"Hello Akash."

Akash opened his eyes and said softly -

"Hey Avni."

"How are you?" Avni was talking very slowly.

"I am fine." Akash replied.

"Are you telling the truth?" Avni asked.

"Yes really. I am fine."

"I couldn't sleep all night." Avni told him.

"Oh, why? What happened?" Akash sat up straight and asked.

"I simply couldn't stop thinking of you - What you must be doing? Are you able to sleep or not? Whether the fever has come down or not. Whether the pain has subsided or not?" Avni went on speaking.

Akash kept listening to her without interrupting. He was realizing how much Avni worried for him. She was able to feel his pain from so far away.

Listen Avni. You shouldn't spoil your own health by worrying so much. See, if I am injured, its naturally going to pain, and my fever is also due this pain. Nothing else. There is nothing to worry so much about. Akash tried to caress her with his words.

"Hmm… you yourself are in pain and you are trying to comfort me," said Avni. "How will you manage your food today?"

"It has been arranged. A man will deliver tiffin at nine o'clock."

"Oh! So, does that mean, you'll have cold food again?" Anxiety was clearly audible in Avni's voice.

Akash shrugged and said, "That's the way things are here. Do I have any other option?"

"If I could control things there, I would have come, prepared food for you and would have fed you myself."

"You would have come all the way here, just to cook for me?" Akash said with a laugh.

"Yes. I would have. Believe it or don't."

"Let it be. I will manage, Avni."

"Please take care of yourself." Avni said in a hushed voice.

"Yes! Avni. I'll take care. You don't worry at all. I'll get better soon."

"Listen, you take complete rest and get some fruits too." Avni said.

"Sure, doc." Akash laughed.

Avni also said in a smiling voice "Ok! Take rest then."

They both laughed softly.

Akash reached the hospital along with Prakhar in the afternoon. The doctor checked the wound and declared that the blood had seeped from the inside of the foot and has accumulated in the sole, so that blood will need to be drained out by making a small incision in the sole, otherwise the infection can spread.

When he returned to the room, it was almost four o'clock. Due to the incision, now the bandage was also tied over his sole. Before today's procedure, he was able to walk a little bit, but now that was going to be almost impossible.

Prakhar had left some fruits and milk in the room. Akash was lying in his bed, feeling the pain spreading all over the leg. He picked up the phone and called Avni, but she didn't answer. Akash closed his eyes and tried to sleep.

His eyes opened upon hearing the phone ringing and saw Avni's call. When he picked up, a voice came from that side -

"Sorry-sorry, I was busy in the lecture. Just saw your call." Avni said.

Akash was still sleepy. He said "No problem" his voice was low due to the pain.

"Akash, are you alright? Does it hurt?" A tone of panic was taking over Avni's voice.

"Today there was an incision in the sole. The blood had frozen there." Akash almost groaned.

"Oh my god. Akash you…" And saying this she hung up the phone.

Akash did not understand why she did this, he sat up a bit and then called Avni. Avni picked it up but didn't say anything

"Avni, why did you disconnect the phone?" Akash asked.

Avni still did not say anything, when Akash listened carefully, he could hear Avni sobbing.

"What happened Avni? Are you crying?"

"No." Avni said and fell silent.

"Something has happened Avni, you are crying, I can hear clearly." Akash said.

"You are alone there..." Avni said sobbing and then fell silent.

Akash remained silent for a while then said lovingly, "Avni! Oh Avni! Don't cry. I know my Avni is a brave girl."

Avni's sobbing did not stop even after hearing Akash's endearments. Akash again tried to stop her from crying, "Listen, my dear Avni. If you cry like such a small baby, then I will stop talking to you. Ok!"

Avni immediately stopped crying and said, "Akash, never say such a thing."

Akash asked, "Ok, I will not say it. But tell me why you cried?"

"You're in so much pain, I can't stand it." Avni said with a twitching nose.

"Arrey... Listen, I'll be fine in two days. Just wait n watch." Akash said in his comforting tone.

"Yeah, I know that you're brave." Avni said.

A smile appeared on Akash's lips. Avni was also comfortable now.

"Listen, when you completely recover, you'll have to do one thing for me."

"What thing?"

"I want your photo. Send me a nice one."

"Hey, I don't have any good photos."

"Don't make excuses, I just want it."

"Ok Baba what will you do with it?"

"Whatever I do, leave it to me."

"Okay, I'll send it, once I get a little better."

"Hmm! OK now you rest. Shall I keep the phone?" Avni asked in a way of asking if he felt like talking.

"Don't disconnect. Let it go on." Akash said with a chuckle.

"I'm keeping. Bye. Please take care, Akash." There was concern in Avni's voice.

"Ok, bye." Akash hung up the phone.

A few moments must have passed after which the phone rang again. He saw Avni's call. He answered and asked -

"What happened Avni?"

"You hung up on me!" Avni said angrily.

"Hey, we did bid our farewells, right?"

"So, you mean you will abruptly hang up on me?" Avni was still angry.

"Oho! Why are you getting angry?" Akash asked.

"No! I am not getting angry." Avni's voice was normal now.

"So, tell me."

"Nothing..."

"Then why did you call, mademoiselle? "

"Just like that."

"One weird girl, you are." Akash said.

Avni did not say anything. Akash further said -

"Now are you going to say something?"

"And will you keep scolding me like this?" Avni said intermittently.

Akash realized that he was really talking to her in an intimidating tone.

"Sorry Avni. I wasn't scolding."

"Don't say sorry. I don't mind your scolding."

"Well then, one dose of scolding every morning and one in the evening. Will it work?"

"Yeah! No matter how much you scold me, I won't mind. Just recover soon." Avni was speaking softly.

"I will be fine in just two days. I promise. May I go to sleep now?" Akash lovingly asked.

"Yes, Akash, you take rest now. And do sleep with your phone close by. Just call me at any time if you feel low. Good night." Avni's words relieved his mind of the pain of his injury for a few moments.

                                    Rendezvous

For the next few days, Avni had created a daily routine of her calls. She would call Akash during breakfast, during lunch or when it was his time to take medicines. Until Akash was busy having his lunch, Avni would talk to him of varied things. If he forgot to take his medicines on time, he would have to face Avni's scolding. She had also explained multiple types of home remedies to Akash, which he would silently listen to and would simply agree with her for the sake of agreeing. Sometimes he would have to note down Avni's home remedies, so that he wouldn't forget them whenever Avni crosschecked with him.

About a week later, the pain in Akash's leg had subsided. Now he was able to use that leg for strolling slowly. Akash's healing had accelerated, not by Avni's strange home remedies, but by her companionship even though she was miles away.

Even though they were physically so far away from each other, their minds had found a way to connect. They hadn't realized the intensity of this phenomenon yet. Sometimes they could convey their emotions without exchanging a word. They had formed and subconsciously accepted an equation between them without having uttered anything about it in words.

As promised, Akash had scanned one of his decent looking photographs and sent it to Avni over an e-mail. Having settled all this, he reached back to his room, the condition of which was like that of a sick man. He started cleaning from one corner and within an hour the room looked much better than before. After taking time off from the cleaning, he opened his laptop and sat down. Prakhar had brought a laptop for him from the office so that he could complete his work from home. He would often play songs or watch a movie on that laptop. He was lost in one of the songs on his playlist.

nayanon mein tere hai sapney

sapno mein hai nasha

ye dil nashe mein behekne laga

tera pyaar dil mein mehekne laga

teri kasam jaan-e-mann

tere bin na lage mera mann

When the phone buzzed with a message notification, he picked it up while listening to the song. Avni had sent a message that she had seen his photo and replied to it over e-mail. Akash immediately opened the mail. Avni had written -

'Akash, you look so good! You have such deep eyes. I couldn't help going on looking into them. The shirt which you are wearing in the photograph, is going so well on you!'

You look smart. I was thinking of sending my photograph to you, but going by appearance, I am nothing if compared to you. If you see me, you might be appalled by the way I look. Please do send more of your photographs.

- Avni '

Akash thought about replying to that e-mail, but after giving it a thought, he picked up the phone and called Avni -

"Yes Akash!" Avni said softly.

"I was reading your mail." Akash said.

"Okay." Avni gave a short reply.

"Okay what ma'am? What all have you written - deep eyes and all?" Akash asked.

"Yes! So, I wrote whatever I thought." Avni gave a quick answer.

"You have misjudged. I don't look all that smart."

"Ok, let it be. You look good, and now you are just being modest."

"I am not being modest. I don't know what you have seen."

"Akash, you look really good. Why should I lie? And no, I will look strange in front of you." Avni said.

"Why are you saying this? Avni, you must be good-looking, because you talk so nicely, and you take such good care of me." Akash caressed her and said,

"Well, you haven't seen me yet. How would you know then?" Avni asked innocently.

"Then you too send your photograph right now." Akash said

"I am not sending any photo. You will make fun of my looks."

"Why are you talking like that, Avni? Please send it. I want to see you now." Akash insisted.

"I don't have any." Avni said.

"So, what? Take a nice photograph and send it to me." said Akash advising her.

"I will see." Avni gave a simple answer.

"Okay, I'll wait then." Akash said.

"Ok."

"Then I'll disconnect now. Some work needs to be taken care of."

"Ok, bye. Take care."

"Take care of yourself too. Bye."

Akash soon got busy with his work. In the background, his mind kept wondering about Avni and things she said about her looks. A few days passed by in these speculations. Akash had now begun going to the office. Whenever he would talk to Avni, he would remind her about sending her photograph.

One night, he was reading something in his room when Avni's message came, stating that she had sent her photo over an e-mail. Akash's heart fluttered with restlessness to see Avni. He had returned the laptop to his office, so he decided to go to the nearby cafe. Looking out from the window, he noticed that the cafe had closed early today. There was no other cybercafe nearby, so he decided that he would go to office early next morning and will check it out.

He suddenly felt that the distance between him and Avni had disappeared. She is right here, near him. With thoughts about tomorrow, he collapsed into the flowing river of sleep.

As decided, he reached office early in the morning. There was no one at the reception. The housekeeping staff was cleaning the office premises.

He went to his computer and sat down to check the mail without any delay. He looked at the unread mail from Avni for a while. Before clicking on the e-mail, multiple thoughts kept passing through his mind. There was a strange restlessness in him as if he was finally getting to see something that he had been waiting for, since a long time.

After saving the photo, when he opened it, he saw a girl with light brown eyes. A slender little nose, thick open hair, cute drop earrings dangling from her ears and a small blue bindi between her delicate eyebrows, matching her salwar. She was sitting in a chair. Her slight smile adorning her fair, simple yet elegant face.

Akash did not know how long he kept looking at the photo. By now, rest of the office staff had started entering the office. It took him some effort to divert his attention from the photograph, so that he could pay attention to his work. In between, whenever he got time, he would steal a peek at the photo. He felt as if Avni herself is sitting in front of him, looking at him, and she will speak now at any moment.

At lunch time, when his colleagues went out to eat, he thought of replying to Avni's e-mail. When he opened the mailbox, there was another mail from Avni in which it was written -

'You must have seen the photo by now, Akash. Whatever you think, please do let me know. Even if you don't like the way I look, please don't start ignoring me.'

Akash could not decide what to reply after seeing the mail. The whole day passed in such a mess. Reaching his room at night, he called Avni -

"Hello." Avni spoke softly.

"What happened to your voice?" Akash asked.

"No, nothing." Avni was still speaking slowly.

"What happened Avni?" Akash asked lovingly.

"Did you see my photo?"

"Yes."

"How is it?"

"Good."

"Meaning?"

"Means it is good, what else?"

"Good." Avni fell silent.

Akash had understood Avni's silence very well, he said -

"You look good Avni. Your eyes are so cute. And the suit that you are wearing in the photograph, is also very beautiful. It looks great on you." Akash said slowly.

"Really? You are lying; Aren't you?" Avni asked.

"No, Avni. Why would I lie? I am telling the truth."

"Let it be."

"No. Really, and those tender lips of yours, I kept looking at them for a long time." Akash let out a deep sigh.

"Really, Akash?"

"Yes! Nothing but the truth."

"And?"

"And what else?"

"You didn't find anything else good in me?"

"Your hair."

"And?"

"Your earrings."

"And?"

"And your lovely long fingers."

"And?"

"That bindi on your forehead."

"Uff Akash, really?"

"Yes."

Avni had fallen silent. Akash could hear her slow breathing. He was lying in his bed. He turned and said softly -

"Avni."

"Yes!" Avni said softly.

Akash did not say anything further.

"Akash." Avni whispered in his ear,

"Tell me, Avni."

"What are you doing?"

"I'm just lying down and you?"

"Me too."

"Okay, tell me; What are you wearing today?"

"Purple suit."

"Have you also worn a bindi?"

"Yes Akash."

"And in your ears?"

"Long earrings."

"Okay!"

"And what are you wearing?"

"T-shirt and jeans."

" Okay!"

"Avni, you look lovely with a smile on your lips."

"You too, Akash. Your teeth are so beautiful. They look like pearls to me."

"Your arms... Those fair arms... They are so smooth, so delicate, Avni."

"Oh Akash!"

"Your hair kissing your cheeks." Akash said while closed his eyes,

"Why don't you come over and brush them away?" Avni's breathing had grown intense

"Your face... I want to enclose it in my hands..." Akash said in an intoxicated voice.

"Yes, Akash!" there was a sense of surrender in Avni's voice.

"I want to feel your cheeks on my palms."

"Oh... Akash!"

"I want to play with your hair."

"Come to me, Akash."

"I'm close to you... So close..."

"Hide me in your arms."

"Avni."

"Yes Akash!"

"Come closer me."

"Akash, I am close to you."

"Come in my embrace, Avni. Press your ear to my chest and listen."

"Oh Akash! I am there with you, my love."

"You are so adorable, Avni."

     Rendezvous

"You too are so handsome, Akash."

"I am feeling an urge to possess you, Avni. I need you."

"I am all yours, Akash."

"Avni..."

"Don't say anything more, Akash..."

Two souls were meeting somewhere in the depths of that night. Their breaths were full of eagerness to embrace and blend into each other, while their passions were soaring. Time seemed to have stopped and it felt as if the whole universe had come to a halt, to treasure those precious moments. Those tender moments were driving them towards a destination where they were companions, they were confidantes.

***

As time passed by, their love was setting up new dimensions. The monsoons were left behind and a mellow coolness had begun to rise in the air. Their closeness had defeated the geographical distance between them.

As if Akash had found a new goal to work towards. Once he was leading a dry life and now with the rise of his relationship with Avni, many changes were clearly visible in him. There was always a glow on his face, accompanied with a pleasant smile.

Love has the potential to induce every moment with happiness and cheerfulness. These characteristics had taken over Akash's being. He found himself caring more for Avni than himself. Where is she? How is she? These thoughts accompanied him constantly. At the same time, Avni too kept continuous track of his wellbeing.

One such day when Akash was busy with some work at his office, he received a message from Avni -

'Are you free?'

Akash immediately called her, "Yeah Avni, what happened?"

"Talks about my transfer are going on." There was concern in Avni's voice.

"What do you mean?" Akash asked.

"I am being sent to a college in Delhi."

"Why?"

"A post is vacant there and they are unable to find another candidate right now."

"Okay then what did you think?"

"Don't know. I am not inclined towards going to Delhi, Akash." Avni said while laughing nervously.

"But you have a house in Delhi. If you stay there, I will also feel at ease. You know, then I won't have these relentless concerns about your safety and wellbeing." Akash explained.

"All that is fine, but from there, I won't be able to talk to you as openly as I do from here," Avni said in a tired tone.

"Oho, so that's the real problem!" Akash said teasing her.

"You... I just don't want to go." Avni insisted.

"Then just talk to the head of your department."

"I already spoke. They are not agreeing to stop the transfer." Avni said screaming.

"I think many good opportunities will open-up for you in Delhi. And moreover, you are also writing a thesis." Akash explained lovingly to her.

"Yes! That's there, but I still don't want to go."

"So now you tell me what should we do? You are not listening to me." Akash almost scolded her.

"See, the way you are talking. Why will I not listen to you?" Avni insisted.

"Then try to accept this change and go to Delhi. Maybe they will call you back later." Akash said

"Okay." Avni agreed but it was clear from her voice that she was uncomfortable with the thought of leaving Nainital.

"Listen." Avni said.

"Yes!"

"Once I am at home in Delhi, I won't be able to talk to you frequently like I do now. There is always a lot of hustle and bustle at home. So, I will call you from my end. You don't call."

   Rendezvous

"Okay! But we can talk at least once a day, right?" Akash asked in despair.

"Yes Baba! How will I be able to live without talking to you?" Avni blushed.

"Hmm! Wouldn't you be able to?" Akash asked teasingly and said, "What if you find someone else there?"

"Oh God! How mean of you? Do you even think before saying such things?" Avni said with a scoff.

"Oho I was just joking. " Akash said with a laugh.

"Let it be, never ever joke like that." Avni said as her voice cracked.

"Avni, sorry dear. I said it just to pull your leg."

 Avni did not reply.

"I am sorry. Please now don't cry over this." Akash said affectionately.

"Promise me that you will never say such things then." Avni said calmly.

"I will not make you cry Avni. Now calm down." Akash said caressingly.

"Yes, I am not crying now." Avni smiled.

"Then where is my kiss today?" Akash asked in a mischievous tone

"Here it is." Said Avni and showered Akash with mock kisses.

Avni had to join the college in Delhi at a short notice of two days. So, she left Nainital the very next day. Since her scheduled time of reaching Delhi, there had been no call from her end. Since she was at her own house, Akash did not have any reason to worry. Avni had sent a couple of messages stating that she was fine, and he should not worry about her.

That day, while returning to his room, Akash bought a nice photo frame from the market, inserted a printed copy of the first photograph which Avni had sent and placed it on the side of his table. Every few moments he would look at it and then with a smile, he would resume his work.

At night while he was preparing to go to sleep, the phone rang with Avni's name lighting up the screen. He picked it up quickly -

"Where were you, girl? It's been five days." Akash said angrily.

"Akash, I have been busy." Avni replied,

"I understand, but so busy that you didn't even call me. And you had asked me not to call." Akash was still a little angry.

"So sorry, my love." said Avni softly

Hearing her delicate tone of voice, Akash's anger dissolved within seconds.

"Are you alright?" she asked

"I'm fine and how have you been?"

"I'm doing good." Avni said

Akash could feel something different in her voice today as if her mind was somewhere else. The usual spark in her voice was missing.

"What's wrong with my little sparrow today? I am missing your chirping voice. Are you not feeling well? Do tell me."

"Akash I'm fine. Don't worry." Avni's voice was still heavy.

"Something has happened. Will Avni not tell her Akash?" Akash said lovingly.

Inhaling deeply, Avni said, "Akash, take me away from here."

Hearing that sentence, Akash suddenly sat up in his place and asked, "What happened? Why are you saying such things?"

"Nothing, you just come." Avni's voice was getting heavier.

"What's the matter, Avni?"

"Akash, when I came to Delhi, I was told that some people were expected to come and see me."

Akash felt a sudden jerk upon hearing this as if someone was trying to snatch Avni and take her far away from him.

"Well then what did you say to your parents?"

"What would I say, I only said that I do not want to get married right now."

"Then?"

"Then everyone started pressuring me stating that my age is passing by and other typical arguments."

"Did you tell them about us?"

"No Akash." Avni paused, then said, "Actually the family which is coming to see me belongs to one of Papa's friends. And his son has known me for a long time."

"Ok then?"

"So, Akash I did not dare to talk to my mother. Looking at the environment at home, it seemed as if she already likes the boy."

"And you?"

"What are you talking about Akash? I can think of no one else, other than you."

"Then you should talk to your mother. Tell her about us."

"Akash, how can I tell her? What should I say? That I haven't even met the boy yet!"

"Hey, but in such a situation, we don't have any option other than telling them." Akash said trying to explain.

Avni stayed silent for a while, then asked, "Akash, when are you visiting your home? You will talk to your parents, right?"

"Yes Avni, I am going on a leave for a week. I will talk to my father about us and then I will ask him to talk to your father."

"Please hurry up, Akash. I don't know why, but I'm feeling really scared." Avni said in a trembling voice.

"That's why I am going. Don't worry." Akash comforted her.

"Take me away from here as soon as possible, Akash." Avni said again in a tired voice.

"Yes dear! I will come soon."

Akash left for his home. All through the way, he kept thinking about how he would present this subject in front of his parents. How would he explain it to them? Even though he is thoroughly aware of the intensity with which his father's dislike towards youngsters indulging in love affairs and inter-caste marriages. He had already made his stand clear, how he considered such methods of marriage as irresponsible acts. Akash remembered how his father had completely cut-off relations with one of their close relatives due to a similar marriage. Despite all this, he still believed that his emotions will be respected, his point of view will be understood, and maybe Papa will agree.

When Akash stepped into the house, he got an unexpected welcomed by his younger sister Dhara. Upon seeing her, Akash asked with surprise,

"What are you doing at home?" In response, Dhara said, "Leave all that, I will tell you later. Come in first."

Akash came inside and touched the feet of his mother and father then went to his room. He was unsure why he felt that the atmosphere at home was a bit sad today. After taking a bath, he heard his mother calling him for lunch. When he came to the dining table, his father was already seated at the table -

"How's it going there?" Papa asked

"Everything is going fine, Papa. How are you doing? Hope your health is fine." Akash asked in response.

"Yes! It's just so-so."

Akash felt something was not normal about his father's response, as if something was on his mind but he didn't probe further. Dhara had not come out of her room yet, so he asked the mother -

"Where is Dhara?"

"You eat, she'll eat later." Mother spoke in a soft voice.

"Okay, but if we had eaten together, we could have talked for a bit." Akash replied while filling his glass with water.

"Talk to her later." Mother answered in a dry tone.

Akash noticed while eating that his father had not given any response when he was talking about Dhara. He felt that something was going on, because of which no one had been comfortable in the house.

He remained locked in his room till evening. In between he talked to Avni and told her that he had reached home and will talk about them today or tomorrow. Many questions were floating in his mind as to how he would begin his discussion. Will he first tell his mother, or will he go directly to talk to his father? He had made a rough outline of how to answer all the question that could rise in different probabilities. Papa used to be in the best mood only while playing cards. The game between them used to go on for a long time and in between they would talk on casual topics. While he was thus immersed in his thoughts, there was a knock on the door.

"Yes! One minute." Akash got up and opened the door. Dhara was standing in front of him.

"So, here you are. Now tell me, fatso. What's up?" Akash teased her.

"See, you have come home just today. If you want me to beat you up, then you can go on calling me fatso n other stuff." Dhara said rolling her eyes.

"Let it be. Don't boast about things you are incapable of doing." Akash said pulling her braid.

"Are you done? Now can I come in?" Dhara came in, pushing him and sat on the bed.

"Why didn't you come to have lunch with me?" Akash asked.

"Well, I had to eat late." Dhara replied flatly.

Akash slid down the chair nearby and asked, "What's going on? Are your studies going well?"

"All is well brother. It's only a matter of few months and then I will become Dr. Dhara." Dhara said with a twinkle in her eyes.

"Oho! Bravo!" Akash said, clapping his hands.

"Well listen, I have to discuss something with you… Err, I mean, I have to tell you something."

"Speak up."

"See! You have to take my side."

"Oh man, what's the matter?"

"Na-Na… First tell me, will you help me?"

"Yes! Have I ever refused you anything?"

"Look, it's serious, I'm not joking."

"Ok! Enough of suspense. Tell me, what's going on?"

"It's just that…" Dhara was going to speak further when mother came inside the room –

"Akash are you free now?" The mother said looking at Akash.

"Yes mother. Do you want me to do something?"

"Come with me. We must get some stuff from the market."

Akash got up and walked out of the room with his mother while gesturing to Dhara that they will talk later.

Mother did not speak a single word throughout the way. Whenever Akash raised any topic while picking up the goods they had bought, she responded in brief answers. His mother's behavior was making Akash feel more and more worried, because she had always been cheerful, and this elongated silence was so unlike her.

After coming back home, when he saw that Papa had gone for the evening walk and Dhara had closed herself in her room. As Akash was stepping towards her room, after placing all bags in the kitchen, mother asked him -

"Did you talk to Dhara?"

"Yes! But nothing special." Akash said, putting his hands in his pocket.

"Okay." Mother gave a short reply and went to the kitchen.

Akash followed her to the kitchen and asked, "Maa, what's the matter? Papa is also not being normal.

Mother kept staring at Akash for a while and then said, "You talk to Dhara."

"Why don't you tell me what's going on, maa?"

"Whatever it is, you go and ask Dhara." His mother said while arranging things they had bought.

"Okay, I'll talk to her." said Akash and then proceeded towards Dhara's room.

Dhara was reading something in her room. He went in, sat down beside her, and said -

"What's going on, Dhara?"

"I was about to tell you when maa took you to the market."

"Yes! So, now tell me."

"Let's go up on the terrace." Dhara said, holding his hand and pulling him.

Upon reaching the terrace, they both settled down near the water tank with their feet hanging. This place had always been Akash's favorite space. He loved to sit there for hours looking at the sky above. The cool evening breeze was caressing his ears today.

"Can we break this suspense now?" Akash asked Dhara.

"Brother, I have a friend in college, I mean my batchmate." Dhara said.

"Yes! So?"

"We really like each other." Dhara said, lowering her head.

"Like as in? What do you mean?" Akash asked staring at her face.

"Dude, you want me to spell out! I mean, we are in love with each other. His name is Mitesh." Dhara said looking at him.

After listening to Dhara's words, Akash stopped moving his feet and then remained still looking up at the sky.

Dhara continued saying, "We have decided to live together, brother. We cannot live without each other. I told this to Papa. Since then, he is not even talking to me, and mother doesn't even look at me. Now you understand their silence, don't you? You must talk to them, brother.

Akash was still staring towards the sky, as if an answer was going to rain down from somewhere up there.

Dhara further said, "He has already spoken to his parents, and we want to get married as soon as our studies are over."

Dhara further went on to talk about herself and Mitesh, about his family, how emotions developed between them, and many other things without taking a pause. On the other hand, Akash was silently listening to her. He could now feel the wind screaming into his ears. That pleasant evening had now turned and come to chew him up. He felt as if someone had slammed him to the ground and now, he was unable to get up.

Dhara shook him and asked, "Brother, are you listening?"

Akash looked at her and said, "Yes."

Dhara heard him, but she could not listen to the pain dissolved in Akash's voice. She went on talking in her own rhythm. Akash went on listening silently to her. In between, he kept saying "Yes" just to confirm that he was listening to her. Dhara was completely clueless of the storm that was brewing in Akash's mind.

They both climbed down from the terrace and went to their respective rooms. Akash sat in the room silently for a long time. With this new knowledge and keeping the heightened sensitivity of the moment in mind, he began making an outline of his point and now he had to do the same thing for his sister. He now had to slice through the cold environment that was emanating from his parents.

Even at the time of dinner, Dhara stayed locked in her room. Papa and

Maa ate quietly, so he too remained silent throughout dinner. Returning to his room, he closed the door and without doing anything else, directly lied down in his bed. He could see the whole room spinning around him. The way last few hours had completely changed the course of his plans, was beyond his imagination. He now had no clue what was going to happen. Amid this turmoil, Avni's message appeared on his phone screen -

'Are you okay?'

Akash couldn't pull himself together to type a reply. He put the phone aside and closed his eyes. Various thoughts were running through his mind. He closed his eyes tightly as if he wanted to bury all his thoughts in there.

Around nine o' clock at night, he left the room and walked over to Papa, sat in front of him and said -

"Papa, I have to talk to you."

Papa looked at him and said softly, "I know what you want to talk about. I don't want to discuss anything about Dhara."

"But Papa, we will need to discuss about it. For how long it will be possible for us to keep a lid over this conversation?" Akash insisted.

"Do you know by now why I'm not talking to her?"

"Yes, papa."

"That's it. Then there can be no further talk on this topic."

"Papa, the matter will not get resolved in this way."

"Why do you think I want to settle that matter? Such things will not be tolerated in this house."

"Both of them are fond of each other and…" Akash was talking, when his mother came from behind and interrupted –

"So, she has sent you to get her point across?"

Akash turned around and saw his mother's face turning red.

"Maa, even if she sent me, it's not as if she has asked an outsider to discuss things, right?" Akash said holding mother's hand and guiding her to sit on a chair.

"Look Akash, you know very well that such a thing like love marriage is not considered respectable in our family. Moreover, he is not even of our caste."

"So, what maa? The boy is a doctor and they have known each other

                                                            Rendezvous

for a long time."

"Now don't play an advocate for Dhara." The anger was clearly audible in his father's voice.

"No papa, I'm not playing an advocate. I am just saying, please listen to her point of view. According to what she told me about the boy, he sounds like a fine match for her." Akash explained.

"Don't you think, you have made a decision too soon?" Mother scolded Akash.

"Maa, you both have to decide. All I am saying is that you call Dhara outside and listen to her with patience. Maybe listening to her whole story will give you some confidence.

"Do you remember what happened a few years ago?" His mother said smilingly.

"You're talking about aunt, aren't you?" Akash said.

"You don't know what condition your aunt is in today." Papa said angrily.

"I know Papa, but it is not necessary that same things should happen with everyone." Akash said looked at his father.

"He also had a good job, was from a rich household, but you know very well what happened later. Your aunt spoiled her entire life because of her stubbornness?" Hints of anger were rising in his mother's voice.

"Yes, everyone knows, but why don't you see that Dhara is an intelligent girl. She will not make the same mistakes which aunt did." Akash said while holding mother's hand.

"Son, people lose their sight, and sense of right and wrong, in these kind of love affairs. Dhara has not even grown enough to differentiate between good and bad." Papa said.

"Papa, she isn't as small as you think. She is living alone outside, managing things on her own." Akash spoke instantly.

"And now you are seeing the result of all that independence; Aren't you." Mother said widening her eyes.

"What have I exactly done, Maa?" Dhara approached murmuring from behind. "It's not like I have eloped with him and got married without telling anyone."

With her words in the air, Akash could see sparks flying in the room. Papa's eyes were turning red, and tear began trickling down mother's cheeks.

"See! How shameless she has become." Mother said almost screaming.

Akash got up and took Dhara to her room and said, "You go now. I'll handle it."

"Yeah! I see what you guys are talking." Dhara cried out.

"Please go in there. I'll talk to them and then will call you outside later." Akash said pushing her in.

"O God! Look at this girl." The mother cried pressing one end of her saree to her lips.

"This insolence won't work in this house." Papa shouted angrily.

"You calm down, your health will get worse." Akash came back and said while sitting beside his father.

"I don't see any insolence in my behavior. What wrong have I done?" Dhara shouted standing at the door of her room.

"Shut up! Go to your room." Mother scolded her.

"I will not go. I must decide today. I have been watching the strange silent drama you both have created ever since I told you." Dhara shouted.

"You shut up for a while. Let me talk." Akash spoke again and gestured for Dhara to return to her room.

"Brother, I have been watching for three days now. Both are engaged in this absurd rhetoric." Dhara said losing her temper.

Upon hearing this, Akash also got angry, and he said to Dhara in a scolding tone, "You are going too far, Dhara. Show a little consideration. I told you that I will talk to Maa and Papa, then why are you shouting?

"Then you just see. They are never going to understand." Dhara said pulling a face.

"Yes! We are just illiterate fools. You are the only wise one in here." Mother said angrily

"Maa, calm down. We will discuss this tomorrow. Right now, everyone is angry. Papa's health will get affected in all this." Akash said explaining to everyone. Dhara stomped her feet and walked away from there, closing the door of her room loudly, she made it clear that this discussion was not going to stop here. Mother also got up and went to another room. Telling his father to go and sleep in his room, Akash left from there.

Akash went to the terrace to let off his steam. He kept wondering how much things had changed at home. He was especially taken aback by Dhara's rebellious tone. Since childhood, she had never fought so boldly for anything. This new form of hers, was a revelation for him.

There she was, ready to go till any length, for her love and here he was caught up in the crossfire, losing all ways to begin talking to his parents about Avni.

Gazing at the sky above, he caught sight of a shooting star breaking away, and merging in the horizon. At the same time, a tear drop rolled down Akash's cheek and merged with the soil below.

Throughout the night, Akash kept tossing and turning. Avni's words and her voice kept coming back to him. He could not talk to her even if he wanted to. What would he say to her? How would he explain this strange atmosphere that had enveloped his house? How would he explain to her that the time was not right for him to talk to his parents about Avni and himself?

He couldn't see any conclusion to the chaos that had filled up his home. Every day he kept thinking about a possible solution, but nothing worked. Next two to three days passed away in this same toxicity. There was no hope for any peace between his parents and Dhara. A seemingly never-ending argument between Dhara and Papa continued at frequent intervals. His mother would just keep crying while pressing one end of her saree to her lips. Akash was trying to balance out and take care of all three in his own way.

One night, when Akash and his father were having dinner at the dining table, Dhara suddenly came out and sat down in front of them -

"What have you all decided?" She asked in a tone which implied that she wanted to take a decision right away.

"What do you mean, what did you decide?" Papa asked looking at Dhara.

"Whether you are going to talk to Mitesh's parents or not?" Dhara said peeping into her phone.

"Dhara, let us eat food first." Akash said scolding her.

"Don't interrupt, brother. You have already tried talking to them in your own way." Dhara said showing a hand to stop him from intervening.

Akash felt a sudden urge to tell her what he was on verge of losing for her happiness. But he remained silent, and tried explaining softly -

"Look, let's talk after dinner."

"I can't wait any longer." Dhara said in a disturbed tone.

"No discussions on this topic now." Papa said shaking with anger.

"Ok. So, I take this as a NO from you all." Dhara stood up with a start as she spoke loudly.

"Yes! Take it that way." Papa said, slamming his hand on the table.

"Well then, it doesn't matter to me, what you think, I will follow my own mind from now." Dhara said with a shriek.

Papa looked at her, struggled out of his chair, picked up the plate and angrily threw it towards the door while saying, "You can do wherever you want, but get out of this house."

Akash got up, grabbed his father's arm, and supported him to sit down. He was breathing profusely, sweating all over his body. Mother got scared seeing this and in anger she slapped Dhara two or three times,

"What kind of a girl are you? You are hell bent on killing your own father!" Mother sat beside Papa giving water to him.

"Yeah, I am leaving. Why should I stay in a house where no importance is being given to the happiness of your own daughter?" Dhara cried out, hitting utensils kept nearby as she went into her room.

Akash was stunned. Such a thing had never happened in this house before. Mother was crying continuously. Papa's breathing was still running fast. Whole house was left cramped with high spikes of sadness and anxieties.

Akash sat next to his father for a long time. When he fell asleep, he got up and went to his mother. She too had fallen asleep. He walked and knocked on Dhara's door. No sound came from inside. Akash called softly -

"Open the door, Dhara. I need to talk to you."

Still no sound, no movement from behind the door.

Akash then called up Dhara from his phone. That too went on ringing for a long time, but Dhara did not answer. By now Akash felt terrified by a peculiar apprehension. He knocked several more times, the stillness from inside was deafening. Now Akash was unable to control himself. He started banging the door and pushing and kicking hard at it. Hearing the noise, mother reached there and seeing him trying to break down the door, she started crying loudly.

Akash kept on trying to break down the door using different methods. Amid all this noise, Papa struggled out of bed and reached there. Upon seeing the fear on Akash's face, he too started hitting the door. Hearing the noise, the neighbors reached the house and when they finally broke down the door, they found Dhara lying on the ground. Seeing the empty vial nearby, Akash understood that she had consumed all the sleeping pills at once. He remembered she was used to taking them often.

Mother was crying loudly, and father was beating his forehead, while sitting on the chair. Meanwhile, someone had called an ambulance. Akash went to the hospital with Dhara and asked the neighbors to take care of his mother and father.

Dhara was admitted to the ICU and the doctors immediately engaged themselves in their efforts to save her. Akash was sitting in the waiting area outside the ICU, when he received a call from his mother that he should quickly come to the floor below. Akash could not understand why his mother had come to the hospital. He rushed downstairs and saw that she was bringing Papa on a stretcher. Seeing this, Akash's heart sank. Somehow managing his emotions, he reached to his mother side. The only thing that came out of the mother's mouth - "Heart-Attack"

Darkness had filled up Akash's vision. He felt as if all the nerves in his brain would burst at once. Dhara upstairs and Papa here... Many disturbing thoughts were passing through his mind. He asked his mother to sit there and followed his father's stretcher which was being carried by hospital staff. Doctors inspected and told that he would have to be kept under observation for the next few hours. Then they will be able to decide whether an operation was necessary.

Life and Death are separated by a thin line of a delicate moment. Every single moment has the power to completely alter one's life. These present moments felt so heavy to Akash that he had lost all sense of self. He got his leave extended for the next several days. Neither did he care about day nor about night. His daily routine was confined between home and the hospital.

Dhara was much better now. When she heard about her father, she kept crying for a long time, but her insistence towards her goal remained. Papa's health had improved slightly. The doctors said that the heart attack was minor, so there is no need for an operation, but it will take time for him to recover completely.

Amidst all these troubles, he got many calls and messages from Avni. He could not pay attention to them, as he was entangled in all these problems. He understood very well that he might not be able to talk about Avni at all. This episode of Dhara's fight for her love had made him understand that if he would talk about Avni, he did not know what else he would have to witness. He diverted his own attention from Avni's topic and remained entangled in the care of Papa and Dhara.

After about two weeks, Papa was brought back home, but he was unable to walk. Dhara stayed in her room. Even after all this, the conversation between everyone had not mellowed down to normalcy. Tension still lingered in the air.

One night Akash was massaging Papa's feet when Papa asked him to sit close to him. Then said -

"You go once and meet the boy." Papa said in a heavy voice.

"I will go and meet him, Papa. But you recover completely first." Tears welled up in Akash's eyes.

"Now I am better than before. You visit the boy and come back. Dhara will also feel secure. Nothing much is remaining of my life. I have lived almost as much as I had to. But her life is yet to begin. If something happens to her, how will I be able to go on living?" Tears had welled up in his father's eyes.

By that time, his mother came and stood beside him, "I had woven so many dreams for finding a groom for Dhara, but it seems God had some other plans." Then, running her hand over Akash's head, she said, "Now all my hopes have taken shelter under dreams of finding a nice bride for you."

Akash's throat grew tight. Sitting there, he was somehow holding himself together. He got up and went to his room, closed the door, and cried hysterically. He was sitting with so many desires. He could see all his decorated dreams falling apart. Avni's face was appearing again and again in front of his eyes. What will happen now? What will he say to Avni? How will he explain all this? Will she be able to understand him? How will this break her? He did not realize, when all these thoughts pushed his tired body and mind into a deep sleep.

Waking up in the morning, he came out of his bedroom and saw that Papa was talking to Dhara. Seeing Akash approaching, Dhara left from there. Papa called him with a gesture and said -

"I have informed Dhara that you will go to meet Mitesh and if his family wants, they can come here and talk."

"Okay papa, I'll leave today, I'll come back day after tomorrow." Saying so, Akash sat up and reached Dhara's room.

On seeing him, Dhara wrapped her arms around him. "Sorry brother! You had to suffer so much because of me!"

"It's okay Dhara. At least they have agreed now." Akash said, placing his hand on her head.

"When are you going to meet them?"

"I'll leave tonight. Do you want to send something for him?" Akash asked looking at her.

"No brother. I have nothing to send. You just bring good news from there." Dhara said, pulling the hair of his grown beard.

"Ouch! So, this is the reward for getting your point across!" Akash said with a chuckle.

"Whatever you ask, brother. I will give it to you." Dhara said while spreading her hands.

Akash saw the happiness sparkling in her eyes, then with a faint smile said, "You have already given me, what you had to give." and left the room. Dhara was so lost in the joys coming her way, that she did not pay attention to Akash's sad smile and tone. Dhara went on losing herself in the bright lights of the future that awaited her, and here something within Akash had extinguished.

Akash came back after having met Mitesh, and his home was buzzing with preparations to host Mitesh and his family members. While Maa,

Papa and Dhara were engaged in preparing for upcoming events, Akash had begun to sink deeper into himself. He would simply do as he was told. Upon their arrival, Mitesh's family members instantly developed a fondness for Dhara. The discussion of engagement and wedding also came up organically in their free-flowing discussions. The auspicious day for their engagement surfaced a week later and it was decided that the wedding would be discussed once both completed their studies.

The engagement ceremony was completed in time. Maa was satisfied that Dhara's would-be in-laws came across as gentle and loving people. Papa also looked happy, but sometimes lines would appear on his forehead out of nowhere. Perhaps the trauma of recent past had left a deep impact on him. Meanwhile, Akash had turned into a lifeless machine. He had wrapped his pain in a fake image of himself. He displayed a smile in front of everyone but had withered somewhere within. He had been trying to shield himself from his own feelings. Many a times, he would sit in his room for hours, lost in his own thoughts, his expressions showing hints of the internal war he had waged on himself.

After about a month and a half, Akash stepped in his small room at Bangalore. He looked around, inspecting the room thoroughly. His moving gaze got trapped on Avni's photograph, which he had placed in the frame on the table, just a few days before leaving. A layer of dust had settled on it. He thought something similar had happened between him and Avni as well. While cleaning the frame, two drops of tears rolled down his cheeks.

Avni's last message had arrived a month ago, in which she had asked him to talk to her. But at that point Akash was not in his own senses, so how would he have talked to her, and what would he have said even if he had called?

Akash cleaned up his laptop, opened it and started checking e-mails. Avni also sent many mails. Her last e-mail was about two weeks ago -

'My Dear Akash,

I don't know what happened to you. Why did you stop talking to me? I sent you many e-mails and called you so many times, but I am afraid you may have been in some trouble, maybe that's why you have not been able to talk.

                                                  Rendezvous

My wedding has been fixed. It's just two days later.

I have been treasuring dreams, that you will come and take me away. I cried so much for you. I am unable to understand, why you are doing this to me! Maybe there must have been some shortcoming in my affection, that's why you have turned away from me.

Wherever you are, this is my singular wish from God, that you be happy. You will always be in my heart. You may forget me, but I will always remember you.

your Avni

Tears had begun dripping from Akash's eyes or were they from the cracks within. He felt as if something had irreversibly broken inside. He sat on the ground pulling his hair and hit his head against the wall. His lips kept repeating -

"Forgive me Avni, forgive me, forgive me, forgive me..."

Day or night no longer mattered to him. His routine had been wrecked by his reckless moodiness. If he felt hungry, he would eat. If he felt sleepy, he would sleep. If he felt tired while working at office, or if his mind wandered somewhere else, he would leave the office to just roam aimlessly in the streets. Now he did not feel like reading or writing anything.

When a man is drained of all emotions, he turns into a walking, talking void. The pain within Akash kept stabbing him somewhere deeper where he couldn't reach and stop those attacks. The smile that used to appear upon his lips was now lost somewhere. His day-to-day life now resembled an apparition.

When someone begins to lead such a dreary life, one either surrenders himself to the devotion of God or hurls himself in depths of intoxication in which he seeks a path to his liberation. Akash soon threw himself in a deep well of work. He began leaving for office as soon as he woke up in the morning and would return to his room very late at night. Even if he left office early, he would reach his room late every night after having roamed around through the city streets.

Prakhar had left his job and had returned to his home in Gujarat. He was now helping his father in his business. In a way, Akash was now all alone and apart from a few acquaintances, there was no one around him whom he could perceive as a friend.

The seemingly infinite series of conversations between Avni and him had met an abrupt end after that last e-mail. After that mail, neither Avni ever sent an e-mail to him, nor did Akash try to write or talk to her. If there was still anything left between Akash and Avni, it was just the memory of many things that had occurred between them and her picture in the photo frame. He would keep staring at that photograph for hours. Sometimes he would smile and sometimes he would cry. Life had brought him to such a point where he had made a habit out of living this way and he simply went on living each day as it came.

***

Akash was entrusted with the responsibility of setting up stalls of his company in the upcoming IT fair. He was wholeheartedly engaged in meeting his goal of turning this little stall into a success story. Such fairs that are held during the end of every year, generally have a variety of events, due to which the company not only got new talent but also got a chance to advertise its products and services in a better way. Akash did not want to fall short in any way. He wanted to execute the work that was assigned to him to the best of his abilities.

Two days had passed in which the fair was abuzz with a lot of activity. People would come to his stall to know about his company and its products. He would oblige them with elaborate presentation about his company. One of those afternoons, he was sitting alone at the stall. Everyone else had gone for lunch while Akash was sitting in front of his laptop doing some work when someone called from behind -

"Hi."

Akash turned raising his eyebrows as if asking without saying anything - "Yes?"

"Sorry, don't mind, but could you please help me?" She asked, brushing her hair back with her fingers.

Akash kept looking at her for a few seconds and then said, "Hmm..."

"Actually, my stall is next to yours, so thought I'd take your help." She said with a nervous pout.

Seeing her pout, Akash smiled slightly and said, "Gee... Sure... Tell me what I can do for you."

After listening to Akash, her lips eased in their natural shape.

"Will you be able to come over to my stall for a while?" She asked, again brushing her hair away from her cheeks.

Akash nodded and followed her towards her stall. When he reached there, he realized that she had been handling her stall all on her own.

"Are you alone here?" Akash asked, inserting his hand in the pocket of trousers.

"Yes! I am alone today. No one else was able to come from office. Work is hectic these days." She said making a face.

Akash stood there looking at her, without saying anything. She was also standing, looking around with both her hands on her waist. After waiting for a few minutes, Akash reminded her and said -

"So, you needed some help; Right?"

Hearing this, she said "Oh! Oh man, such a fool I am." And giving a sarcastic pat on her own back, and then a quick slap on her own head, she continued, "I am unable to setup this inverter. Can you please help me with it?" She said while sitting near the inverter, tapping on it.

Akash signaled her to move away from there with a gesture of his hand and then went to the inverter and started inspecting it. After a while, he completed the setup and sat down on the ground. He raised his head and saw that the girl was missing from there. He got up and went outside the stall and looked around. She was nowhere around. So, he brushed both his hands and went back to his own stall.

He had just relaxed back in his chair, when the girl entered his stall in a hurry. She had a bottle of cold drink in each hand and was out of breath.

"Oh sorry! I had gone to get this for both of us. She swayed the bottles between her fingers and spoke. "Is it working now?"

"Yeah, it's done." Akash replied sitting down.

"Oh! Thanks. I tried but was somehow unable to do it." She said laughing.

Akash looked at her. She was pointing a bottle to him with an outstretched hand, gesturing him to take the bottle. He said -

"You need it more than I do. Looks like you went running to find it!"

"Oh yes! I thought you are helping, so I owe a small treat to you." She said shaking her head.

"I don't drink cold drinks." Akash replied with a smile.

"Oh ok. Right... I just drink around two or four of these every day." She said while sitting in a nearby chair.

"Okay" Akash said looking into the laptop.

She remained silent for some time, as she had devoted all her attention to drinking her cold drink. Then she said, "Well, will you drink tea?"

"Yes." Akash again gave a brief reply.

"Then let's go to the canteen, I'll treat you to tea there." She said getting up from her chair.

"And this other bottle?" Akash asked, pointing to the second unopened bottle.

"Oh! don't worry. I will finish this one too." She replied with a laugh.

Akash looked at her white teeth and said, "I am busy now. We'll have that tea some other time."

She stood there thinking for a few seconds and then said, "No problem, my stall is just next door. We can have tea at any time." Saying this, she walked towards the exit of the stall, but paused and said,

"So sorry! I didn't even ask for your name."

"Akash."

"Ok. My name is Sakhi." She smiled lightly while saying this and then made her way to her stall.

Akash too got busy in his work. He returned to his room quite late that night at about eleven o'clock. Entirely fatigued, he lied down in his bed and started looking at something on his phone. After lying down for a while, he got up, changed clothes, then moved the chair and sat down resting his hands on the table. The same photo frame glared at him, but there was no photo in it. He had taken out the photo and had hidden it somewhere in his belongings. Perhaps by doing this, he wanted to convince himself that even though he will always have her, she is not his.

He sat down at his table and kept looking at that empty photo frame for a long time until his eyelids drooped. When his sleep broke after midnight, he got up and went to the bed to lie down. But like many other nights, his sleep had defied him tonight as well, and had fled somewhere else.

The next day his stall was overcrowded, as he and his accomplices were taking profiles of candidates who had just passed out of college. This continued throughout the day till evening. When he got a little free, he came out of the fair and stood by a tree. He was standing silently looking around, basking in the waning twilight of the evening, when someone put a hand on his shoulder.

"Hello!"

Akash looked back and saw that Sakhi was looking back at him with a smile on her lips.

"Hi." Akash replied softly.

"Done with today's work?" Sakhi asked, swaying her fingers left and right.

"No, I wanted a break so just came here for a while." Akash said, crossing his hands in front of his chest.

"Oh, good." Sakhi nodded.

"What are you doing here? Have you taken a break as well?" Akash asked

"Arrey, no. I was coming back from office. I had just parked my car and was walking towards the fair tents when I saw you here. So, I just thought I will meet you." She paused for a while and then said, "You don't mind my intrusion; Do you?"

"Oh no, not at all." Akash said straightening his posture.

Both stood there in silence for a while. Akash was looking up at the scattered colors of the sun setting in the sky. Sakhi was also silently looking around at the trees. Sakhi cracked the silence between them -

"The weather feels so nice today; Doesn't it?"

"Hmm." Akash shook his head slowly while looking up.

"I like to spend time on my terrace, listening to songs on such evenings." Sakhi said taking a deep breath.

"That's nice." Akash again shook his head slowly.

Sakhi looked at Akash. He looked as if he was searching for something in the sky. Looking at him for a while, she asked -

"So, you live alone here?"

"Yes! I have got a room on rent." Akash had lowered his head and was now leaning with his hand on the tree.

"Okay, and what about your family?" Sakhi asked.

"Papa, maa and my sister. She got married recently." Akash replied.

"Okay." Sakhi paused again and said, "I am the only daughter of my house. I hail from Lucknow.

Akash looked at her and said "Okay" and smiled.

"How about some tea?" Sakhi asked with a slight tilt of her head.

"Hmm! No. Sorry. I must get that job done. Some other time." Akash replied and turned to walk back towards the stall.

Sakhi also joined him. Both were silent while walking. Akash was lost in himself, and Sakhi kept looking at Akash every now and then.

"See you soon then." Sakhi said turning as she reached her stall.

"Yes! Of course." And Akash proceeded from there and walked towards his stall.

Sakhi was watching him leave. A small smile had appeared on her face as she entered her stall.

From the next day, Akash could not attend the fair. He had to take care of some unfinished office work which was waiting desperately for him. The response to the fair had been good. Everyone at office had been praising Akash for his skilled performance at the fair. On the other hand, Akash was disinterested in any kind of praise. If someone would come and congratulate him, he would say "Thanks" to him and then go back to his work.

The next few days went on like this. Akash would keep himself busy so that he never got time to revisit his memories, thus dodging the pain they had in store for him. One such day he was busy working at office when a call from an unknown number flashed on his phone. When he answered the call, a voice from the other side said -

"Hi."

Akash could not recognize the girl's voice and said "Who?"

"Oho! Sakhi here."

"Oh Sakhi! How are you?"

"I'm cool. And you?"

"Fine."

"Don't ask where I got your number from."

"Oh yes! Where did you get it?"

"Took it from your stall."

"Ok."

"Okay listen, I called so that I can invite you."

"Meaning?"

"That means your tea is still pending. So, I thought that you should be called and offered tea." Sakhi said with a smile.

"What's the occasion?" Akash asked.

"It's my birthday party. Will send the venue details, reach on time."

"Oho! But I..." Akash had begun saying but was interrupted.

"Come on please." Sakhi insisted in a baby like voice.

"I will try." Akash said.

"I will wait." Saying so, Sakhi hung up the phone.

Akash had been running away from social gatherings since a long time. He had stopped going to any casual event. His world was confined between his room and his office. He had almost given up meeting anyone. He used to avoid attending the office parties on one pretext or another. He was feeling a little uncomfortable after that call from Sakhi. He could not understand how to refuse her.

On next night, at eight o'clock, he reached the address which Sakhi had given. It was a cozy little restaurant. Sakhi hadn't invited many people. There were just 7 to 8 people including him at the table. He was feeling hesitant with this scenario where he would be expected to socialize. Sitting at one corner of the table, watching the rest of the people dancing and singing, his gaze turned to the twinkling lights outside and the sound of singing and dancing was bouncing off his ears.

A gleeful laughter echoed in his ears. -

"Happy Birthday Akash. May you live for a thousand of years, and may each year consist of fifty thousand days."

That night came back in front of his eyes. Avni had called him up at midnight to wish him. She was so happy, and for she had sung on the phone for so long. He didn't even realize when Sakhi had come and stood in front of him.

"Hello. Hey Akash. Are you meditating or something?" Sakhi asked cheerfully, "I have called your name twice already!"

"Oh sorry." Akash said calmly,

"Can we cut the cake now?" Sakhi smiled and asked.

"Yes, yes, come on." Akash quickly got up and went with her.

After a while, Akash went out on the lawn with his plate of food. There was no one else around. He took a sigh of relief and found an empty chair lying nearby. He sat in it. After a few minutes, Sakhi came out with her plate and settled down in a chair next to him. Seeing her, Akash smiled lightly.

"Why are you sitting here alone?" Placing her plate on the table, Sakhi asked.

"No, just like that." Akash said without looking at her.

"You don't like to attend parties; Don't you?" Sakhi asked, leaning towards her plate of food.

Akash remained silent for a while then said, "I have come to a party after a long time."

"Okay, you mean you rarely go to parties." Sakhi said while eating.

"Yes! Just that I feel a little uncomfortable in crowds."

"So, you like your solitude." Sakhi said pulling her chair near to the table.

"Don't know. Yes, maybe." Akash said nodding.

"How do you do that? Don't you feel bored?" Sakhi asked shrinking her eyes.

"You know Sakhi, everyone's life is not the same." Akash's eyes deepened.

                                                      Rendezvous

Sakhi saw Akash's face and then fell silent. Both did not talk till the end of the meal. Akash kept eating silently, staring at his plate, and Sakhi's eyes kept moving towards Akash's face again and again.

By the time the party got over, it was eleven o'clock. Everyone had left. Sakhi asked Akash to drop her till her apartment. Akash too thought that it would not be right for her to go alone so late at night. Both were silent while Akash rode the bike. A lot was going on in Sakhi's mind, while Akash was also lost in his own thoughts while driving. When they reached Sakhi's apartment, she got down from the bike and said to Akash -

"Thanks Akash."

"It's ok, Sakhi." Akash smiled lightly. He was about to turn his bike when Sakhi said -

"Akash, of course not everyone's life is the same, but at least an effort can be made to make it better."

Akash raised his eyes and for a few moments he kept gazing into Sakhi's eyes. With a slight smile on his lips, Akash pushed his bike forward. Sakhi stood there watching him disappear from her line of vision.

When Akash entered the room, that same chirping voice reverberated in his ears "You live for a thousand years..." He pressed his ears tightly with his hands and collapsed in his bed. The tussle between sleep and Akash went on all through the night.

Almost a month had passed since the night of Sakhi's party. He and Sakhi had grown to talk often over the phone. Sakhi would tell him about little things going on in her life and would try to make him laugh with her absurdly funny jokes. Akash had no hesitation in talking to her, but there was still something inside him, that wasn't allowing him to connect completely with anyone else.

"Listen, Akash will you like to go on a trip with us?" One day Sakhi asked him while talking over the phone.

"What kind of a trip?" Akash asked flatly.

Hearing his tone, Sakhi said expressing her annoyance, "On a mountain. Will take you there and will push you."

"Why do you need to go that far to push me?" Akash laughed.

"Dude, you are not the sporty type at all. What are those words... Yes...

You are mean and rude." Sakhi said teasing him.

"Whatever... I won't go." Akash replied by imitating her tone.

"Please come along. How much do I have to plead in front of you, man?" Sakhi said.

"Where are you going?" Akash asked.

"There is a place named Antargange. We will go on a night trek. We will start the trek there at 10 o'clock in the night and reach the top around 4:00 in the morning." Sakhi explained in detail.

"Okay, and when will you come back?" asked Akash, resting his hands on the table.

"We can climb down by stairs while coming back. It will take twenty to thirty minutes. And then we can come back immediately."

"Hmm."

"What hmm! Are you coming?" Sakhi said in a loud voice.

"Let's see." Akash exhaled.

"Look, you are coming and now I am not going to listen to any of your excuses." Sakhi said with authority over him.

"Okay man, when is the program?" Akash asked.

"Tonight." Sakhi replied with a cheerful laugh.

"What time?"

"Eight o'clock. We will be leaving by a minibus. We will pick you up from the bus stop near your house."

"Ok." Saying this, Akash hung up the phone.

While boarding the minibus, Akash looked around till the back seat of the bus. Except for Sakhi, it was full of unknown faces. It was a group of twelve people, and all were probably Sakhi's colleagues. Sakhi gestured with her hand to the one of the girls who was sitting in the back seat to move a bit, making space for Akash, who then settled in the other corner of the back seat.

While trekking, Sakhi was walking in front of Akash and turning back again and again, while talking to Akash about worldly matters. There was an appropriate arrangement of lighting throughout the trekking path. However, everyone's steps were progressing slowly. After going a little

                                    Rendezvous

further, Sakhi was climbing on top of a big rock, when her foot slipped, and she fell backwards. Akash was right behind, he held Sakhi and supported himself by leaning on another rock behind him.

"I told you so many times to look ahead while climbing." Akash said still holding her, waiting for her to take control of her balance.

"Sorry-sorry." Sakhi's weight was completely on Akash. She regained her balance and she said, "Oh man, my mistake."

The rock on which Akash had leaned, had left a scratch on his hand. Sakhi grabbed his arm and said -

"Show me. So sorry Akash, you got hurt because of me." Sakhi was trying to remove the dust from the wound by blowing over it while looking at Akash every now and then.

"Come on, it's not as much as you are making it out to be." Akash said, releasing his arm from her grip and started moving forward.

"Yes! Okay. Now you go ahead and if you slip, I'll save you." Sakhi said innocently.

Akash laughed at her tone and moved on. Sakhi was watching him climb upwards. Her eyes sparkled even more in the light there.

When they reached the top, Akash and Sakhi looked at the glistening lights below and smiled at each other, appreciating the beauty of the view. They sat there in silence for a while, lost in their own thoughts. Having spent some time there, everyone started climbing down using stairs made of stone slabs. Coming down didn't take much time. They boarded the minibus at around five in the morning. There was still a lot of time to leave. Akash entered the bus and saw that the back seat was completely empty. Everyone had occupied the front seats. It was probably the effect of tough lessons the rocky road and potholes had taught them on their arrival journey to the foot of the mountain. He went and sat in the back seat.

Sakhi hadn't boarded the bus yet. Akash peeped out of the window and looked around, but she was nowhere to be seen. He had just pulled her phone out of his bag to call her when he caught sight of her boarding the bus. She came straight to the back seat and sat beside Akash

"Arrey, shift a bit and sit there. The whole seat is empty. You are sitting almost on top of me!" Akash told her while gesturing with his hand.

"I am not going to bite you." Sakhi said showing her teeth, "And I want to sit there by the window."

"The window seat on the other side is empty. You can go there." Akash said in Lucknowi dialect.

"Sire, this is where I am going to sit by this window. Come-on, move a bit." Sakhi replied in the same dialect. As she pushed him aside and captured the window seat. "See, got it." Sakhi said showing her big glistening eyes.

"Ok, sit here then. I will go to the window on that side." Saying so, Akash grabbed his bag and tried to get up. Sakhi grabbed his hand and pulled him back saying - "Sit here quietly."

Akash looked at her face and then sat there by her side. The bus had left the rocky path and was now running on plain road by now. Since everyone was tired, the driver had switched off all the lights inside, so that anyone who wanted to sleep could rest for a while. It was going to take about two hours to reach the city, so Akash also closed his eyes and rested his head on the backrest.

"Will you take me there in the mountains? We will sit there and see clouds floating below us."

"Sure. Wherever you say, my love."

"Then take me there. Why don't you take me there, Akash?"

Dense smoke had engulfed the mountains and he was unable to find Avni anywhere. He shouted - "Avni, Avni..."

"Avni!" Akash was mumbling in his sleep.

"Akash! Akash!" Sakhi shook him by his shoulder.

"Hmm." Akash opened his eyes. He saw Sakhi holding his hand and shaking him. He stood up and looked around inside the bus as if searching for something. Then he sat back in the seat and bowed his head down.

"Akash, are you ok? Did you see a bad dream?" Sakhi asked, still holding his hand.

"Dream." Akash said softly.

"And what were you mumbling? Avni, Avni?" Sakhi asked placing her palm on his shoulder.

"Nothing, it was just a dream." Akash said turning his face towards Sakhi.

                                          Rendezvous

Sakhi looked deep in Akash's eyes. They were heavy with tear drops, which he himself was unaware of. Sakhi smiled lightly and said -

"Ok…" She took her hand off his shoulder and reclined back in her seat.

Akash was looking at the light peeping in from the windows, moving inside the bus as it moved ahead. At the same time, many questions were rising in Sakhi's mind. Along with her thoughts, her eyelids too grew heavier, and she fall asleep. However, sleep couldn't find its way back to Akash's eyes.

A mellow cool breeze was coming in from the window. There was still some time for the morning to take over the dark night. Sakhi's head had slipped from the backrest and had found a resting place on Akash's shoulder. She was sleeping, with her arms crossed around her shoulders, trying to guard herself from the periodic blasts of cold air. Akash slowly opened his bag, took out a shawl and covered Sakhi with it. In between when she opened her eyes lightly, she saw a shawl over her. She smiled in half wakefulness and again let herself fall into the lap of sleep.

At the bus stop near Akash's room, as she watched him descend, Sakhi said – "Take care of yourself, Akash. Make sure, you sleep well at home."

Akash got off the bus nodding his head in response to Sakhi. The bus started and she kept looking out of the window, watching Akash go.

No one knows when life decides to give something, or when it decides to change something. Sakhi felt in that moment that today she had received something. Her mind was filling up with some strange sensation. A little sapling of love had taken birth in her mind.

It was Saturday. Akash was in the library, immersed in some book, when the clock stroke eleven o' clock. His legs kept shaking continuously without him being conscious about it, while he sat in a chair taking notes in a diary. His phone screen brightened up with a message notification –

"Can we have a call?" Sakhi had sent.

Akash had asked her to avoid calling on mornings of Saturday and Sunday, as he is often in the library, and she could send a message if there's something urgent.

Akash messaged back "I will call in a while."

When he returned to his room, it was twelve o'clock. Cradling his phone between his ear and shoulder, he called up Sakhi, while undoing the laces of his shoes.

"Now tell me." Akash said

"Got time finally?" Sakhi said taunting from the other side.

"Hey man, what's the matter?"

"Come home."

"Home! Are you crazy?"

"Oho… come on… There is no one at home."

"What do you mean by - nobody?" Akash was a little stunned.

"Arrey, I'm alone. Room partner has gone out. She won't return before night. Come, I'll cook some scrumptious lunch for you. Such, that it will be impossible for you to forget the flavors throughout your lifetime." Sakhi said perkily in one breath.

"Really! And your landlord? Will he let some boy enter his property?" Akash asked teasingly.

"That's the best part. Even he is out of town." Sakhi said effervescently.

"I'm not coming, man." Akash had now straightened up taking the phone in his hand.

"Be careful of your choices, dear. You are about to miss some serious food made by one of the best chefs in the world all over again." Sakhi said with a mock pride in her tone.

"That's not the point, Sakhi. If your landlord comes to know later, it will not be right." Akash said explaining to her.

"Leave all that. I'll take care of all that," said Sakhi, assuring him.

"Some other time then." Akash said trying to avoid.

"Hey listen. I am alone, it does not mean that I will rape you. Come quietly till one o'clock, understood?" Sakhi said, rebuking him.

Akash couldn't help laughing at this -

"Okay ma'am. Now I am feeling safe. Since you have promised that you will not rape me, I will come over."

"Yes! Come soon, I'm waiting for you." Sakhi said and disconnected the call.

Akash had reached Sakhi's apartment at around one o'clock. Sakhi's flat was on the second floor and the flat next to her was that of her landlord, with a big lock hanging. The door to Sakhi's flat was open. Mellow vocals of a ghazal were trickling out from a music system indoors. He called out from the door itself -

"Sakhi!"

Sakhi came out of the kitchen, "So, you are here finally! Come in." She gestured him with her hand to come in.

Akash stepped in and walked towards the dining table. He slid a chair out and sat down. Sakhi had cleaned up the house and placed everything neatly. On one side was the sofa set. The dining table was in the middle and the music system was in a corner behind him. The enticingly smooth melody of ghazals had filled up the room.

He was looking around the room, when Sakhi fetched water for him and sat down in a chair beside him

"So, how are you doing, janaab?" Sakhi said in her Lucknowi dialect.

"I am breathing, living - all by your grace." Akash replied in the same dialect, bowing his head.

Akash's made-up tone triggered Sakhi's giggles. She got up from there and started moving towards the kitchen.

"You had left the door open. Amazing!" Akash said sarcastically.

"So? I was expecting you. Is there something about you that I should be afraid of?" She asked with a laugh.

"If someone else would have come?" Akash teasing him asked.

"So what? I would have seen what to do in that scenario. You think, I am afraid?" Sakhi asked with a knife in her hand,

"Okay, put away that knife, I don't know about you, but I am afraid." Akash said with a sarcastic grin.

"Hey, don't you dare underestimate me; Ok?" Sakhi said shaking her hair.

"Well, well... Leave all that aside. Is the food ready or not?" Akash asked looking towards the kitchen.

"Absolutely… Everything is ready. I was just waiting for you." Sakhi said, wiping off the sweat from her forehead.

"Yes! I can see that you are working so hard." Akash smiled.

"Yeah, so what? You will be eating food cooked by me the first time. It has to be perfect." Sakhi said shrugging her shoulders.

"Then what are we waiting for?" Akash said, getting up from the chair.

"Wait man, first tell me, how am I looking?" Sakhi asked while standing and turning around.

Akash put his hand on his waist and looked at her from top to bottom. He realized for the first time that Sakhi was beautiful in an unconventional way, a kind of attractiveness that emanates from a beautiful mind. He didn't know when his casual viewing turned into a thoughtful gaze.

"Where is Akash Babu lost?" Sakhi asked snapping her fingers.

"Hmm! You look ok." Akash said, pulling a face.

"Just, okay?" Sakhi said, her eyes growing bigger and rounder,

"I mean you are looking good." Akash said going towards the washbasin.

"If you are saying so, I must be looking good." Sakhi said.

"Okay, now what's this logic?" Akash asked while washing his hands.

See. You are such a serious type of a person. You are so lost in yourself that you don't even look at pretty girls around you. Considering all that, if a person like you says that I look good, then it must be probably true." Sakhi said with a laugh.

Akash shook his head drying his hands with a towel and sat down at the table "Your logics are as strange as you are. It's above my capacity of understanding. And what do you mean by, I do not see anyone?"

Putting food items on the table, Sakhi said, "Yes, so tell me, have you ever taken any girl on a date yet? I have not even seen you looking at any girl in the way boys normally look."

Akash smiled silently looking at her.

"Don't smile." Sakhi said staring at him. Then sitting in a nearby chair she asked him – "Go on, tell me, have you ever taken someone on a date?" she said with mischief dancing in her eyes.

"Leave that topic, yaar." Akash said patting her head.

"Arrey tell me. You might have liked someone if nothing else." Sakhi asked teasingly.

"Give it a rest, Sakhi." Akash said pulling a face,

"Ok Baba! What can one even ask you?" Sakhi said getting up from the chair, then she went to the kitchen to get the rest of the things.

Akash was struggling to keep himself from getting lost in thoughts.

They discussed various subjects while eating. Ghazals, songs, books, and many other stories from their respective lives. After having finished his meal, Akash got up and reclined on the sofa -

"Sakhi, the food was too good. Ate a bit too much of it though."

"So? That was expected from you. After all, who had cooked it?" Sakhi asked, brushing her hair back,

"I had so much of it that I am not even able to move." Akash said holding his stomach.

Sakhi laughed and said, "Now get ready for dessert. There's a whole cake. I can see just one person who I can feed it to."

Akash folded his hands and said dramatically in a pleading way, "Forgive me O' mother. Consider me incapable of eating any further."

Sakhi laughed out loud and fell on one of the sofa chairs.

"I am feeling sleepy now." Akash yawned and said, "I will go home and enjoy a sound sleep."

"Hey, you will travel all the way till your room to sleep. By then your sleep will evaporate. Do one thing, go and sleep in my room." Sakhi said, placing her feet on the table.

"Are you crazy? In your room, that too in your bed. You say anything without thinking." Akash said rubbing his eyes.

"Oho! Akash… Ok, do one thing. Go in the room and lock it from inside. I won't try to come in and rape you." Sakhi giggled.

"Sakhi yaar, can you ever be serious?" Akash shook his head.

"And can you ever be normal sometime?" Sakhi said picking up the cushion kept nearby and throwing it towards Akash.

"Really? Is it ok if I sleep in your room?" Akash said, with his eyebrows raised.

"All yours." Sakhi said closing her eyes and shaking her head,

"Okay but wake me up in an hour." Akash said going into the room.

"Ok boss." Sakhi said with a salute.

Akash must have been asleep for a few minutes. Sakhi peeped into the room and saw that he was in deep sleep. As Sakhi was closing the door slowly, she heard something. As if Akash is saying something in his sleep. She went inside and stood near the bed.

'I will come and will take you away with me, Avni.'

Akash was mumbling lightly. Hearing that name, Sakhi remembered about the instance in the minibus. At that time too, Akash was mumbling the same name. When Sakhi sat beside him on the bed, she saw a few drops of tears slip out from Akash's closed eyes. She kept looking at him silently for a while, then she kept her hand on Akash's head and began to caress him.

Akash sat up in bed and upon seeing Sakhi, he asked with a shocked expression,

"What are you doing in here?"

"You were going on mumbling something in your sleep. What were you talking about, Akash?" Sakhi asked him.

"I don't know... maybe I must have dreamt something." Akash said running his palm over his face.

"No Akash. You were mumbling the same name which you had taken in sleep on the bus the other day." Putting her hands on Akash's knees, Sakhi said,

"What name? What are you saying?" Akash said looking away from Sakhi's questioning eyes.

"Avni." Sakhi said softly.

Akash suddenly fell silent as if he had forgotten to breathe. He was still looking away from Sakhi. Rubbing his forehead, he slid backwards in bed.

Sakhi moved closer to Akash and looking deep in his eyes, she asked, "Who is this Avni?"

                                          Rendezvous

Akash's tongue couldn't move, as if it had got stuck in his mouth. Tears welled up in his eyes. He was still trying to avoid looking back in Sakhi's eyes. He paused and said, "No one."

"I can't believe that she is no one, Akash. There is something that you buried deep in your heart and that seems to be slowly consuming you from within." Sakhi said keeping her hand on Akash's hand.

Akash turned and looked at Sakhi. A couple of tears rolled down from his eyes and flowed down his cheeks.

"Tell me what happened, Akash." Sakhi said looking into his eyes.

Akash closed his eyes and, nodding his head, leaned back against the wall.

"Akash, I want to know please tell me. You can trust me. That's what friends are for." Sakhi said, sitting close next to him and taking Akash's hand in hers.

Akash opened his eyes and gazed in Sakhi's eyes for a long time. Then sitting upright, he said -

"I have caused a lot of pain to her... to Avni..."

"How? What had happened, Akash?" Sakhi said, placing her hand tenderly on Akash's cheek.

Akash looked at Sakhi and said, "I love Avni a lot... but now she is not with me anymore."

"What do you mean?" Sakhi asked.

"She left. I don't know where she must be now?" Akash's voice had turned heavier, so he paused.

"Ok, I understand it's difficult for you to talk about it. But go on... You need to share whatever is hurting you so much." Sakhi asked, pressing his hand.

"Everything has been left behind a long time ago. It doesn't matter anymore." Akash said in a heavy voice.

"Whatever it is, Akash. I want to know." Sakhi said while stroking his hand.

Akash then went on narrating how he first interacted with Avni. How love bloomed between them. How they grew closer with each passing day. He narrated everything sequentially as everything was happening right now before his eyes. Then as he spoke about those nights at his home when everything scattered to pieces, he began sobbing profusely and mist had gathered in Sakhi's eyes too while listening to the intensity of Akash's words.

After he had told her everything, they sat together in silence for a long time, then Sakhi wiped her tears and said -

"Akash you are very lucky, that you were able to experience moments of such deep love. What you told me is so full of innocence, that it feels divine. And I too am also lucky to have a friend like you." Sakhi said looking at Akash.

Akash was looking at Sakhi. His eyes were still wet. Sakhi took his face in her hands. Akash put his head on her shoulder and wept as if floodgates of a dame somewhere inside him had opened. When Sakhi put her hand in his hair, two drops falling from her eyes fell on Akash's cheeks.

Weeping like this for a while, Akash suddenly got up and started walking out of the room. Sakhi was still holding his hand. She pulled him back and made him sit on the bed - "Where are you going now?"

"Back to my room." Akash said wiping his tears.

"I will not let you go now. Are you aware of the state you are in?" Sakhi said while placing her hand on his shoulder.

"I will need to go, Sakhi. I cannot keep sitting here." Akash said getting up.

"Right… You will go to your room and then roam around reddening your eyes further." Sakhi said scolding him.

"So, what shall I do?" Akash said with a smile.

"Akash, sit here and listen to me." Sakhi said while making him sit again.

Akash sat down said, "Now please don't start giving any lecture."

"Akash, I have no interest in giving you any lecture. All I have to say is that if she is never going to come back in your life, what's the point of going on mourning? I know you both experienced the purest form of love together. But now it has been a long time since all that, Akash. Life is all about moving forward. By living like this you are slowly destroying yourself. Don't do this to yourself. You deserve your own share of happiness." Sakhi said while explaining to him.

"Whatever it is, how can I forget her? She didn't go of her own free will. It was my fault that we aren't together." Akash said with a restless annoyance.

"Look Akash, I think it was nobody's fault. You both faced certain circumstances simultaneously, on which both of you had no control over." Sakhi said trying to comfort him.

Akash looked at Sakhi and said, "Suppose you were in Avni's place, how would you have felt? Wouldn't you think that I have failed in taking any efforts to stay together. Or worse, wouldn't you think that I have fled away with the fear of getting married to you? Tell me?"

Sakhi remained silent for a few moments and then said, "Akash, I can never take Avni's place. My heart keeps sinking just thinking about what she must have gone through. But I am just saying that why are you torturing yourself by remembering those things now. Well, tell me, can Avni come back to you now?"

Akash was sitting silently. His head was bowed down. He was staring at the floor with such intensity as if all answers to Sakhi's question were written down there somewhere. After a few moments had passed in silence, Sakhi shook him and said -

"Akash you should move on now. You cannot forget everything that happened, but you can try to make peace with memories of those times by not blaming yourself, because by doing so you are treating yourself unfairly."

"Hmm... I don't know." Saying so, Akash fell silent again.

For some more time, both again stayed silent. Akash got up abruptly and left the room. Sakhi also got up and followed him. Akash picked up his car keys and before exiting from the door of her house, he paused for a few moments and then left. Sakhi followed him to the door and with moist eyes, she watched Akash drive away.

That day, the little sapling of love which had sprouted inside Sakhi, had grown up, flexing its branches in her soul. She wanted to drive Akash out of his misery and for that she was ready to take all kinds of efforts. As days passed, she took him out for dinners and movies or for strolls in parks, on some pretext or another. She would spring out strange jokes on him out of nowhere. Akash couldn't help giving in to her insistence. But the one thing that remained alive was Avni's love. No matter how much he tried to hide it, it would occasionally surface on Akash's face. Which she could not erase even if she wanted to.

As days were passing by, Akash kept receiving repeated calls from home, to meet a girl, which he would avoid every time by making one excuse or another.

On the other hand, Sakhi's conversations with her family members had completely stopped, ever since she had made it clear at home that they should not look for boys because she had no intention of getting married. After repeated questions about why she doesn't want to get married, Sakhi clarified that she has already chosen the one whom she wants to marry but the boy doesn't know about her feelings yet. After getting to know this madness of hers, her family members would taunt her on every phone call, which she would bear by countering them with her jokes. Her mind was concerned with just one thing - how to tell Akash how deeply she loves him. How was she supposed to stop memories of Avni from haunting him? For Sakhi, her days and nights had taken the form of Akash.

***

Akash was busy with his work at office that day. Loads of work had arrived on his table at once. His phone rang with Sakhi's name displaying on the screen. He answered, pressing it under his ear and said while looking at the computer screen -

"Yes Sakhi."

"Are you in the office?" Sakhi asked.

"Where else can I be?" Akash gave a simple answer.

"Ok, can you leave the office early in the evening?" Sakhi asked.

"Why is there something special?" Akash questioned.

"It's nothing special, but tell me, will you be able to leave?"

"I will try."

"Tell if you can leave office for sure."

"What's the plan?"

                                                      Rendezvous

"I'll tell you when we meet."

"Hmm okay. Where should we meet?"

"How about the coffee house opposite to your apartment?" Sakhi replied after thinking a bit.

"Ok done" Akash said, disconnecting the call.

He reached the coffee house around seven in the evening. To his pleasant surprise, it was sparsely crowd. His eyes wandered around the café, looking for Sakhi, but there was no sign of her anywhere. He pulled up a chair at a nearby table and settled there watching something on his phone when Sakhi arrived and sat in the chair opposite him.

"Man, there was too much traffic today." She said in a complaining tone.

"That's the usual scene, madam." Akash said teasing him.

"Yeah, I know." Sakhi replied irritably.

"So, will you bother to tell me, why you called me here?" Akash spoke again in a teasing manner.

"Dude, let me breathe a little." Sakhi said slapping Akash's hand.

"Will you have coffee?" Akash asked.

"Yes, a coffee would be great. Ok, listen, I am hungry too." Sakhi said in a demanding tone.

"Ok." Saying so, Akash went towards the counter and returned after placing the order. As soon as he sat down, Sakhi asked, "Will you come to Nainital with me?"

Akash felt a shock in his spine as soon as Sakhi had uttered the word 'Nainital'. He looked at Sakhi speechlessly.

"Please don't refuse." Sakhi said with folded hands.

"Why should we go there?" Akash asked softly.

"Oho! I remember now, man. That's your favorite place too." Sakhi said with a laugh.

"But why should I go there? And that too with you?" Akash again asked.

"With you! What does it mean? Do I bite you or something?" Sakhi said angrily.

"Hey Sakhi, come-on, don't be angry." Akash said.

"Ok, tell me, why do people go to a hill station?" Sakhi shot her question.

"Obviously people go to hill stations to unwind. But, why there of all places?" Akash asked.

"I want to go there. That's why." Sakhi said, pulling a face.

"Then you go with your friends." Akash looked at the counter and replied,

"Yes, two of my juniors will be coming along." Sakhi said to him.

"Good, so what's the problem?" Akash asked.

"You too have to come." Sakhi said in an assertive tone.

"Oh man, you have begun your chase now." Akash said with annoyance.

"Yes, take it that way. You will have to come." Sakhi said retaining her assertive tone.

"Dude…" Akash had started saying something when Sakhi interrupted, "Look, I am requesting you so much. You have to just pick your bags and come along."

Akash paused for a while and then he agreed still a bit reluctantly.

Sakhi told him the whole plan and said, "Apply for leave in advance."

Akash was lying in his room. Many voices had been echoing in his mind all through the day. A string of old moments would keep rocking his thoughts back and forth. All this restlessness had kept his mind in a state of turmoil.

He got up and dragged out an old bag from under the bed. There was a lot of dust on it. It was clear from its condition that he had left it like this for a long time. Opening the bag, he took out an old diary of his. The same diary which he had scribbled many songs and poems. Opening it after such a long time, gave him a glimpse of the old days. After turning a few pages, his fingers stopped on one page. He slowly read the lines there –

शहर ख़ामोश गलियाँ सूनी सूनी सी लगती है

ज़िंदगी ठहरी हुई सी सुकून भरी सी लगती है

                                                           Rendezvous

इस वक़्त जब रुक गया सब अपनी जगह
तन्हाई में भी नहीं कोई कमी सी लगती है

ये खुदा का करम है या है कोई सज़ा बता
जो भी हो जिंदगी फिर हसीं-हसीं सी लगती है

The city seems silent, the streets feel deserted,
life must have paused to take a leisurely breath,

in this moment everything has paused in its place
there's no lack of anything even in this loneliness,

is it God's doing or is this some punishment,
whatever it is, in here persists the beauty of life

A strange expression appeared on his face while reading it. To shake away his discomfort of coming face to face with himself from another time, he turned the pages of the diary. His eyes fell on another poem -

तमन्नाओं की बारिश अब थम सी गयी है।
कुछ इस कदर जिंदगी रुक सी गयी है॥
तुम लौट आओ तो मौसम फिर जवाँ हो-
वो चाहत की आग कहीं बुझ सी गयी है॥

the rain of desire is at a standstill now
life has taken a pause in such a way,
if you return, this season will grow young again -
the flame of desire will stay cold till then.

After reading it, he put the diary aside and then took out a large envelope from the bag. When he turned it upside down, Avni's photograph floated down to rest on the bed. There was also a piece of paper in which something was written. He picked up the paper and read it -

दुश्वारियाँ दिलों की है कुछ ऐसी
सुलझाना उन्हें आसाँ तो नहीं है
थक गया हूँ तकदीर से लड़कर कि
बीते दिन ले आना आसाँ तो नहीं है
और फिर बैठा हूँ हारकर यूँ कि
तुम्हें भूल जाना आसाँ तो नहीं है

such are the plights of the heart
it isn't easy to resolve them,
fighting my destiny has left me weary
it isn't easy to bring back the past,
after having lost i have settled here
it isn't easy to forget you, my love

Since he had written this poem, he hadn't written anything. Akash was holding Avni's picture in his hands. He was caressing it with his fingers. As if he wanted to ask, 'How are you, Avni?'

As the night grew dense, silence spread everywhere, but Akash's ears were filled with simultaneous echoes of various voices. He pressed both his ears firmly with his palms, closed his eyes and cocooned himself in his bed.

It was time for the train to leave and Sakhi had not arrived yet. Akash was standing outside, looking around, waiting for her to appear in midst of the crowd. He saw her running towards him. Akash took her luggage and hurriedly followed her into the train. The train had begun to leave the platform.

After occupying the seat, he asked, "Hey, why did you take so long?"

"It was a mess. I had to pay the autorickshaw driver, but somehow my purse was nowhere to be found." She said while fixing her hair.

"Hmm." Akash said softly. Then asked, "And where are those two companions of yours?"

   Rendezvous

"They are in the next bogie." Sakhi said while placing her luggage safely.

"Ok, why didn't you reserve their seats here?" Akash asked.

"They wanted to sit together." Sakhi replied.

"Yeah, so? They would have been together in this compartment as well." Akash said, opening his shoelaces.

"My dear friend, try to understand people's need for personal space sometimes." Sakhi said widening her eyes.

"Oh, so that's the scene. Ok, got it." Akash said with an expression of delayed realization on his face.

, "Yes, that's the scene." Sakhi said, "And listen, when they come here tomorrow in the morning, don't keep staring at them."

"What do you mean? Do you think I roam around staring at lovebirds?" Akash asked.

"That way, I know, you always stick to your own business. But still don't sit around interrogating them. I have told them about you. That you are an ultra-serious kind of a man." Sakhi laughed while speaking. "Their names are Mukul and Preeti."

Akash smiled softly and lay down on his berth. He looked at Sakhi. She was looking at him. She smiled softly and started looking for something in her bag. Akash lying down said -

"Sakhi, whenever you feel like having your meal, just wake me up. I am feeling very tired, so will take a quick nap."

"Ok, you rest." Sakhi blinked her eyelids.

Akash closed his eyes. Sakhi looked at Akash's face and kept gazing at him for a long time. Then she closed her eyes and rested her head against the window, letting herself immerse in some thoughts.

After having their dinner, Sakhi fell into a deep sleep, while Akash was engrossed in thoughts, tossing, and turning in his bed. When he opened his eyes in the morning, he saw that Sakhi was not on her berth. The train was standing at some station. Akash felt that Sakhi might have got down on the platform. He got up brushing his clothes with the back of his hands. While he was looking for a toothbrush in his bag, Sakhi came from behind and sat down on her berth. Akash turned around and caught sight of the glow on Sakhi's wet face, while small droplets of water in her hair glistened in the sunlight straining in from the window.

"Where had you gone?" Akash asked

"I had just stepped out to wash my face. The restroom was engaged." Sakhi replied smiling.

"Okay, then I'll go out and brush my teeth." Saying this, Akash moved towards the exit door.

"Hurry up! The train can leave at any time." Sakhi's voice came from behind.

When he returned after brushing his teeth, Sakhi had arranged for tea. He smiled at her and said, "Thanks."

"Yeah, it's ok." Sakhi said making a face.

Looking at the steam emanating from the tea, Akash was again lost in some thoughts. Sitting there for a while, he kept looking out of the window. His attention was broken by Sakhi's voice.

"Will you have some biscuits?" Sakhi asked showing a packet in her hand.

Akash took out a biscuit and started eating it after dipping it in tea. The journey was long. Sakhi and he kept discussing various topics. In between, Mukul and Preeti also kept joining and leaving at will. They also contributed with their views on some topics.

The next morning upon reaching Nainital, they went straight to the hotel. Sakhi's head started hurting due to the fatigue of the journey, so she went to bed in her room. Mukul and Preeti were at the reception enquiring about nearby places worth visiting. Akash threw his belongings in the room and set out to the Naini lake.

After roaming around for a few hours, he returned to the hotel and got to know that Sakhi was looking for him.

"Where were you man?" Sakhi asked angrily. "And you left the phone in the room?"

"I went down for a stroll to the lake." Akash said softly.

"At least you could have told me. I have been looking for you since so long." Sakhi said expressing her annoyance.

"Sorry." Akash said holding his ear.

Sakhi laughed and said, "Well, let's eat something and then we'll go explore a bit."

"Ok I'll take a shower and will see you in the restaurant" said Akash while going towards the room.

After having breakfast, both left for Mall Road. They had lunch there and after roaming around two or three places, they came back to the hotel in the evening. At night everyone gathered in Mukul's room and their rounds of gossip, poetry recitals, funny tales, ghost stories continued till late in the night.

Late at night Akash returned to his room and went straight to bed but sleep kept defying his eyes. He got up, sat in the chair, and kept looking at the moon for a long time. He lost awareness of time and then his own senses as sleep stealthily crawled over him. When he woke up with a start at around three o'clock in the night, he got up, went to bed, and lied down.

Waking up in the morning, Akash again went out without informing anyone and roamed around the town. He had left a note at the reception that he would return after having his lunch outside. He returned at three o'clock and went straight to have a bath. When he came out and was getting ready, the phone lying on the table rang.

Akash answered the phone call.

"Where are you?" Sakhi asked.

"I've just returned. I'm in the room." Akash replied.

"I am sitting here on the lawn of the hotel. Come over here."

"Are you sitting alone?"

"Yes! Preeti and Mukul are not back yet."

"Okay, I'll be there in a while." Akash hung up the phone saying.

He had spent the whole day roaming through streets of Nainital. He had begun to feel a little tired. It was four o'clock in the evening and the weather outside was pleasant. With the thought of enjoying the sips from a cup of tea, he set out towards the lawn. Sakhi was sitting at a corner table on the lawn and was calling him to that side with a gesture of hand. Akash waved his hand and walked towards her.

The lawn area was open from two sides. The view was blessed with expansively stretched out tall Himalayan ranges. A few small clouds floating here and there were adding to the idyllic charm of the view and the clear weather.

As Akash sat in the chair, he inhaled the cool air, and then looked at Sakhi who was looking at him.

"Yes, tell me now?" Akash said.

"Dude, have you come all the way here to sit inside the room or to enjoy the weather?" Sakhi asked, almost scolding him.

"Both." Akash smiled.

"You think, you are doing some sort of favor for the whole Nainital?" Sakhi asked teasingly.

"Oh no man, I was tired, that's why I went straight to the room." Akash explained.

"Okay, all right." Sakhi finished the talk and said, "Well listen, you will have some tea; Right? I have ordered it."

"Now that you have ordered already, let's drink it." Akash said.

"What's the plan now?" Sakhi asked.

"I don't have any plan in my mind. I've been walking around town all day." Akash said resting comfortably in his chair.

"Where all have you been roaming by yourself all day? We could have gone together." Sakhi said.

"Just like that." Akash said, looking at the distant hills.

"Dude, you are weird. Who roams alone like that?" Sakhi asked making a face.

"I do." Akash said looking at Sakhi, who was still staring at him. Akash looked at her and smiled slightly.

"I know, you like being alone." While taunting, Sakhi further said - "Listen, there is a sunset point nearby, will you come?"

Akash thought for a while then replied "You go with Mukul and Preeti"

"Both of them have already left. They will meet us there. And I want you to come with me. I will not go on my own." Sakhi said in an assertive tone.

"Dude, the car is here, the driver can take you there directly." Akash explained.

"I am not going alone. You are going with me. That's all." Sakhi was now adamant.

Akash looked at Sakhi who was sipping her tea and was gazing for something in the hills, to avoid looking at him. He understood that she was angry and was trying her best to show that.

Picking up his cup of tea, Akash said, "Ok, let's go then."

Sakhi placed her cup of tea on the table and said looking in Akash's eyes, "Listen, don't try to showcase that you are doing some sort of favor on me."

"And you don't try to showcase that you are angry. It's obvious that you are acting." Akash laughed.

"Lower down this attitude of yours in front of me." Sakhi said, showing her teeth.

"Ok I will try." Akash raised his eyebrows and said, "So, at what time are we going?" Akash asked.

"We will leave in a while. It takes 20 minutes to reach there. It's an amazing place. You will like it too.

"Alright, I will get ready and will meet you in the lobby downstairs." Akash said getting up and walked towards the room.

"Fine then! But listen, not the lobby. I will wait for you near the car." Sakhi said as she got up.

"As you wish, my lord." Akash saluted as he left.

Sakhi laughed. She kept watching Akash walk away. Her eyes were gleaming as if some wish of hers had come manifested itself.

During their drive to sunset point, Akash's eyes were relishing the illusion of tall trees running in the opposite direction. He was sitting by the window and his face was being bathed by gusts of wind. While passing through these roads, something was going on in a corner of his mind. He was lost in his own thoughts, while admiring the views of the valleys all around.

Sakhi would sometimes look at the road in front, and sometimes at the distant hills. She looked at Akash who was still lost somewhere outside.

She started observing his expressions, trying to read his mind. Whatever time she had spent with Akash in the last few months, it was clear to her, that he was a restless soul. Ever since they had arrived in Nainital, he was not at ease. She could understand the reason for that.

In about twenty minutes, they reached the entry gate of Sunset Point. The vehicles could go up to the top, but Akash said, "Since the peak is quite near, let's go by foot." Sakhi told the driver to park, and both got down from the car.

Akash was walking silently on the path towards the hilltop. Sakhi too was also silently observing Akash. Covered in silence, their walk ended in a few minutes as they reached the top.

The blowing wind and the beauty of the surroundings were at their peak. The evening twilight had glazed the environment around them in pleasing colors. Green valley filled up their view as far as eyes could see and the clouds were floating over the peaks in such a leisurely way, as if they too had come there with an intention to find peace. In midst of all this, Akash still lost in himself, walked around for a while, and then leaned by a huge boulder.

Sakhi stood a little ahead of Akash and was observing the view all around. She turned towards Akash and said -

"The sky looks so magical from here; Doesn't it?"

Akash looked at Sakhi and nodded, 'Yes' and then smiled looking at the distant mountains. Sakhi went near and asked -

"What are you smiling about, Akash?"

"Nothing, just at a stray thought." Akash said with a long breath.

"Well, won't you tell me?" Sakhi asked while going closer.

"Can you see those high mountains there!" Akash said, pointing with a finger.

"Yes." Sakhi said looking at him.

"They have been standing like that for ages, at the same place. They have not moved from there even a bit." Akash said.

"Yeah, so?" Sakhi said while agreeing.

"As if their time has stopped at one place and they are always living in this moment. For innumerable years they will continue living like this."

Akash said looking at Sakhi.

"Why do you think so much, Akash?" Sakhi said looking at him.

"It's more than a habit for me. If I don't think, I may as well not exist." Akash said, leaning back on the rock. "My life too has become like those mountains. It is always at one place every day, just like the previous day."

Sakhi looked at him thoughtfully and said, "You know, Akash… If you pay attention to the springs that flow from the middle of these mountains, they carry away all the restlessness that the mountain holds within."

Listening intently to each word of hers, Akash kept looking in her eyes for a long time.

Sakhi further said, "You should also express whatever goes on in your heart. Don't keep it all within like that."

Akash moved his gaze from Sakhi's eyes and resumed looking at the mountains. Their conversation was interrupted by ringtone of Sakhi's phone. She stood up, answered the call, and left while telling him that she will come back in two minutes. Akash thought, Mukul or Preeti may have called, trying to reach out to them. He remained sitting there on a large stone as he watched her go.

It had been quite some time since Sakhi had left. Akash looked around, trying to find her, but she was nowhere to be seen. He thought, she might have walked farther away while talking. He again turned his attention towards the mountains, while thinking on lines of Sakhi's analogy about the streams.

A few minutes had passed when his phone rang. He picked it up and saw Sakhi's name on his screen. Looking around to see if she was nearby, and convinced that she wasn't anywhere around, he answered the phone -

"Where have you gone?"

"I am here." Sakhi replied softly - "Listen, remember we saw a huge old tree while walking towards the sunset point? Come to that tree."

Akash, while looking for the tree, asked "Why all the way there?"

"The view from here is too good. The sun will set in a while, so this place is apt to relish it."

"Hmm... Sounds good. I'm coming." Saying so, Akash hung up the phone.

There was a vast old tree with its branches stretched across the sky, at the other end of the hilltop. Akash started walking in its direction. When he reached there, Sakhi was nowhere to be seen. He stood there for a while and turned around in all directions looking for her. There was no one else around. He pulled out the phone and dialed Sakhi's number. After a few rings, a voice came from the other end -

"Hello."

The voice was not that of Sakhi. Akash looked at his phone screen to check if he had dialed the correct number. There was nothing wrong with the number. He placed the phone back on his ear and asked, "Sorry, can I talk to Sakhi?"

After a pause from the other end, the same voice filled up his ear, "Akash!"

This time he found the voice to be familiar. Suddenly he felt a bright light filling up every nerve and then flashing up his mind. He could not utter a single word.

"This is me… Avni…"

Suddenly, his feet trembled, as if the ground had started shaking. Listening to that voice, he unconsciously moved backwards to find something he could support himself with. His back touched the trunk of the tree. He could see everything moving around him. Tears had begun dripping from his eyes. Words felt caged in his chest, and his tongue felt as if it was imprisoned somewhere in his mouth.

There were no words from Avni's end either. Akash remained still reclining against the tree, with the phone still on his ear. He had closed his tearful eyes trying to get a hold on himself. He felt as if someone was standing on the other side of the thick tree trunk.

Taking the phone off his ear, Akash leaned back to see none other than Avni standing in front of his eyes, with Sakhi's phone in her hand. Akash found himself to be incapable of processing all this in one go. While his mind was struggling to deal with this shock wave, his phone slipped from his fingers, tumbled, and stopped near Avni's feet. When Akash looked up, he saw Avni keeping Sakhi's phone in her purse and leaning down to pick up his phone. As she was picking it up, she stumbled. Akash

     Rendezvous

immediately stepped forward to hold her hand, and by supporting her with his arm, he took her to sit on a stone bench adjacent to him. This was the first time Akash and Avni had felt each other's touch on their skins.

Such are the peculiar ways of nature. The first touch had added a spark to the innumerable emotions flowing within them. That touch had a life of its own and its vigor was felt by both, but this momentary touch was insufficient, to eradicate the distances which had spanned days, weeks, months, and years.

"Are you alright, Avni?" Akash asked while sitting on the stone bench with her. He still could not believe that it was the same Avni whom he had loved with everything he had within him.

"I'm fine, Akash." Avni looked up at Akash, then lifted her dupatta and fixed it in its place.

Akash looked at her carefully. She was wearing a brown suit. Something similar to the one she had worn in the photograph she had sent to Akash. Words came out of his mouth -

"After so many years!"

Avni said adding further, "After four years, Akash."

"Four years have passed!" Akash said in a dowsed voice and then became silent. He raised his eyes again to look at Avni's face. She was now looking at the distant mountains. Observing her frail frame, Akash realized that she was not keeping well, so he asked -

"You are not feeling well; Right?"

"Yeah, I arrived here last night. Since then I have a slight fever." Avni said softly.

Akash almost scolded her - "And you have come alone here, that too in this condition!"

Avni smiled and replied, "That's good. You can spend our time today in scolding me." and then tears formed in her eyes.

Akash looked at her and said softly "Sorry I did not mean to scold you" and then lowered his eyes.

"You look so weak. Are you okay, Akash?" Avni asked while taking out water from her purse.

"Yeah, I'm fine." Akash could not conjure up courage to meet her eyes.

"Why are you lying? There are dark pits under your eyes, and the thickness of your stubble, makes me wonder when you had your last shave." Avni said expressing concern.

"Nothing has happened to me. It's just due to too much work at office." Akash said, rolling his eyes.

For the next few moments, both remained silent. Akash was still sitting with his head bowed. Avni was watching him and was waiting for Akash to say something. When she could no longer bear the silence, she broke it saying -

"Akash, look at me please."

Akash was pressing his fingers. It was clear from his body language that he was not comfortable in front of Avni. He had kept his eyes lowered.

Avni said again - "Please look at me and talk, I have come here only to meet you."

Akash slowly raised his head and their eyes met.

His own voice echoed in Akash's mind -

'Ah these eyes, I used to spend hours gazing in them, living the life of my dreams in them. This endearing, innocent face, which I had lost all my consciousness to, when I had beheld it for the first time. Even now this face has that same glow.'

Both looked into each other's eyes and set out on a journey through distant memories. Those days, those nights, a series of never-ending conversations. Those beautiful moments in which they had lived together, took care of each other, loved each other. They were reliving every single memory in these few moments. The pain and happiness of the past were reflecting in their eyes.

As strong winds blew around them, two souls had risen from their bodies, floating, swaying with the wind, to blend with each other. The flame of desire kept twinkling in their eyes. Without saying anything, without listening to anything, both expressed their pain to each other.

Their eyelids were now finding the burden of pain too heavy to bear. Drops rained down from Avni's eyes. Seeing her tears, Akash, who was still trying to keep control on his emotions, couldn't help letting go of the downpour of tears.

Avni wiped her tears off her face. Akash also calmed himself down. Those compassionate moments had lightened their hearts to some extent.

"Has anyone come with you?" Akash asked.

"Yes! Mother has come. I told her that I am going to college, and that I will come in the evening. So, she is waiting for me at the guest house." Avni said.

"Have you resumed teaching in the same college?" Akash asked.

"No, there was a get-together of the old staff, to which I was invited."

"So, are you still teaching in Delhi?"

"Yes, and now my thesis has received an award." Avni said proudly. Now she was a little comfortable.

"Oh wow! Congratulations, Avni! I am so happy for you." Akash smiled and said, "I too had joined another company after..." Akash told her.

"I know, Akash." Avni said interrupting him.

"How?" Akash asked in surprise.

"Sakhi told me everything about you." Avni picked up Sakhi's phone and handed it over to him.

"Sakhi! Do you mean you both know each other?" Then he said after thinking for a few seconds, "Obviously, that's why she must have given her phone to you." Akash said in astonishment.

"Sakhi called me about a month ago," Avni said with a smile.

"But where did she get your number from?" Akash asked.

Avni said, "One day, I received a mail from Sakhi. She had written that she wants to talk to me. I shared my number and asked where she got my e-mail id from. She told me that she got it from your laptop. You must have casually left it open sometime." Avni smiled softly.

"Oh! So, Sakhi planned all this!" Akash said patting his head.

"Yes, and she told me everything that happened to you and what all you have been going through." Avni said.

"Is that why she planned this Nainital trip?" Akash asked.

"I had told her that I would have to go to Nainital. Maybe she planned your trip accordingly." Avni said with a smile.

"Oh! Ok." Akash said softly and then fell silent.

"And she also told me why you suddenly stopped talking to me." Tears filled up in Avni's eyes again.

"What did she tell you?" Akash asked.

"Everything about the way events took shape at your home, when you had gone there to talk to your parents about us." Avni said, wiping tears from her eyes.

"Oh! so she has told you everything." Akash closed his eyes and said with a frown.

"Please don't say anything to her." Avni said, "It is because of her, that I have been able to meet you today."

"Hmm." Akash shook his head.

"I'm sorry, Akash. You had to go through so much pain because of me." Avni said lowering her eyes.

"It's not at all that way, Avni. It was not your fault." Akash said consoling her.

"It was my fault, Akash." Avni said with tears. "If I hadn't come into your life, you wouldn't have to endure all this."

"Avni, you were, are, and always will be the most beautiful part of my life. So, please don't cry. I can't see you crying like this." Akash said wiping his eyes.

"You are giving me this pep talk, as if you are not crying." Avni said looking at Akash lovingly.

"Look, where am I crying now?" Akash said with a fake smile on his face.

"I caught one of your weaknesses." Avni said with a laugh.

"Really! Which one?" Akash asked, remembering something.

"Do you remember? You used to catch my weaknesses." Avni asked with a smile.

"Oh yes!" Akash said with a fond smile of remembrance.

"In the same way, I know when you are faking a smile." Avni spoke in a cheerful tone.

Akash remembered those early days when both met for the first time over a chatting application.

     Rendezvous

He laughed softly, looking at Avni, who was watching him carefully.

"Your teeth are still like pearls." Avni said.

Akash remembered, Avni had said this often whenever she was on call with him and if her eyes would fall on his photograph at the same time.

"Why wouldn't they be, ma'am. All thanks to *Dabur's Lal Dantmanjan*." Akash said repeating his reply, in the same old tone.

Both burst out laughing. This one little laughter made both feel lighter.

For a while, both did not say anything and kept looking at the clouds floating above the distant mountains. Searching for something in her bag, Avni took out the small box and extended it towards Akash. He asked with a gesture of his eyes what was in it.

"Open and see." Avni said with a smile.

When Akash opened the box, there was *Gajar ka Halwa* in it.

"Oh wow. Gajar ka Halwa!" His eyes widened and looking at Avni, he said, "You remembered?"

"How can I forget Akash?" Avni said while giving him a spoon. "Take this and eat it completely. I made it with my own hands." She said chirpily, "I somehow managed to arrange for carrots in the guest house this morning and prepared it. Avni said looking at Akash lovingly.

"Thank you so much for this, Avni." Akash shook his head.

"Please don't say thank you. I have that much of a right on you." Avni said and then continued, "It must have cooled down, so it may not taste as good."

Taking out the *halwa* with a spoon, Akash said - "Anything made by your hand will be delicious." And then he took the first bite. While chewing, he closed his eyes as if every morsel in his mouth, was elating his soul into a state of nirvana.

At the same time, Avni was smiling contently just watching him eat. Two drops of tears spilled from her eyes. There was an immense joy of satisfaction brimming from her face.

Akash shook his head, and said while opening his eyes, "Man, this is amazing" and then he pointed with his finger and asked for another spoon.

Avni nodded her head and replied that there is no other spoon. Akash then took the *halwa* in a spoon and extended it towards Avni saying, "We should eat this together, though I have used this spoon."

Avni looked into his eyes and said, "That's ok with me." and Akash fed the *halwa* to her with his hand.

While taking that bite, Avni felt as if she had absorbed a small part of Akash within her. She closed her eyes, rested her head back and sat down as if she wanted to live that moment to the fullest.

When Akash saw her doing this, he asked, "What happened Avni? Are you okay?"

Avni opened her eyes and smiled softly towards him, "I am fine."

Then Akash busied himself in relishing the rest of the *halwa*. He kept the box aside and asked Avni for water. After drinking water, Akash said -

"I have something that I want to show you" and he stood up. Putting his hand in his pocket, he took out his wallet and sat back.

Taking something out of the purse, he showed it to Avni and asked, "Do you remember this?"

Avni looked closely and saw it was a handmade wrist band. That day flashed before her eyes. How she had brought all the necessary goods from the market and had woven it with her own hands while staying awake through the night.

"How can I forget, Akash? I had made this with my own hands and had sent it to you." She said taking that band in her hands.

She remained silent for a few moments while caressing the band, and then she said to Akash with wonder in her voice, "You have saved this till now!"

Akash nodded his head and said, "Everything that you have given me, I have saved it with me." There was a slight sign of water in Akash's eyes.

Avni raised her head and said looking at Akash, "Why don't you forget everything now?"

Akash did not answer, and he kept staring at Avni as if trying to say - 'How can I forget you, Avni? Is there a way you know of?'

Avni asked him to extend his hand. Akash slid forward a little and put his hand in front of her. Avni tied that band on his wrist and then sat back.

Akash was caressing the tied band and Avni was gazing at Akash.

"Can I tell you something, Akash?" Avni asked softly.

Akash shook his head in affirmative.

"What do you think of Sakhi?" Avni asked directly.

"What kind of a question is that?" Akash asked, snapping his fingers.

"Tell me, how do you feel about her?" Avni insisted.

"She's a good friend." Akash turned his neck to the other side and gave a flat answer.

"I know, she is just a friend to you. But does she see you just as a friend? Avni asked.

"What do you want to say Avni?" Akash was now shaking his legs. It was clear from this that he did not like this topic being conversed between them.

"That have you ever tried to understand her beyond her role as a friend?" Avni insisted.

"What can there be with her, other than friendship?" Akash said in a single breath, with clear annoyance in his voice.

Avni said, "Look at me, Akash. I know you have always seen her as a friend. But what I have seen in her eyes when she talks about you, is something far more than friendship."

"Meaning?" Akash asked.

"She loves you with all her heart." Avni said explaining to him.

"Impossible" Akash said loudly and stood up.

"If you don't want to believe me, Akash, don't believe it, but I have seen it clearly. There was so much respect and love for you in her eyes." Avni tried explaining to him again.

"Why are you doing this?" Akash asked.

"Because you have to stop wasting your life like this." Avni said angrily.

Seeing this tone of hers, Akash remained silent.

"Why do you keep hurting yourself like this? I can't see you like this, Akash." Avni said, then she slid a little closer and said to him, "Not a minute has passed without your thoughts in my mind, for all these years. I have always been worried for you. I keep wondering about your wellbeing.

I keep thinking, what would you be doing? Now that we have met today, I cannot leave you like this. Avni paused for a while and then said further "You must start your life afresh now. In this way neither you will be happy, nor will I ever find peace. There will always be a feeling of guilt in my heart."

"Stop it, Avni" Akash said interrupting her. "It can never happen to me again. I can never feel all those emotions for anyone else."

There was silence for a few moments between them. Then Avni asked, "Akash today I want to ask you something. Will you give it to me?"

Akash looked at Avni's face and then silently said with his eyes, 'I can sacrifice anything for you, Avni. Whatever you ask for, will be yours.'

Avni said, "Let Sakhi take care of you. She will be with you for her whole life. She will love you a lot."

Akash was speechless. He closed his eyes and kept his head bowed down.

"Akash, you are precious to me. I don't want to lose you to this void that our relationship has left." Avni said while placing her hand on Akash's hand. "Move ahead, Akash. Be happy and may you achieve many successes in life - I pray this every moment and will continue to pray thus throughout my life."

Akash raised his head and looked into Avni's eyes. By shaking his head lightly, he tried to show that he would not be able to do this.

"I know how difficult it is for you," said Avni, pausing for a while. "No one can erase what was between us. But we can't ever stop living; Can we?"

Akash's face became teary-eyed. He shook his head and said, "Avni I will not be able to do this." as if his heart was bleeding inside him.

"You have promised. Your Avni is just asking you that you live well, that you find happiness again. Can't you give me even that much?" Tears welled up in Avni's eyes.

Akash could not stop himself. He got up and sat next to Avni. He began to collect the scattered pearls on her cheeks. Avni closed her eyes. As Akash's hand was wiping her tears, she placed her hand on Akash's hand and cushioned her cheek with it.

There was silence all around, as if time had paused, stopping the winds coming from the mountains. Both were living in these moments like nothing else existed around them.

Avni pressed Akash's fingers with her fingers, then opening her eyes, she looked at him with a question in her expression, 'You will fulfill your promise; Won't you Akash?'

Two drops of tears fell from Akash's eyes. Looking deep into Avni's eyes, he accepted her demand without saying anything.

Water gushed out from Avni's eyes; this time accompanied with a smile of contentment.

"What a heavy burden you have lightened from my heart!" Avni said, wiping away her tears.

Akash remained silent, as he was now busy trying to prepare himself for parting ways with Avni again.

Avni further said, "You should always be happy and keep Sakhi happy too, tell me, will you do this?"

"Yes Avni." Akash said softly.

The wind was getting stronger now and the sky had started to darken. Akash, looking at the shadow descending on the distant mountains, asked Avni,

"When will we meet again?" There was pain in Akash's voice.

Avni remained silent for two moments then said, "I don't know Akash."

Just like sky and earth create an illusion of meeting somewhere at the horizon, destiny may have decided something similar for Akash and Avni.

The colors fade. Days also keep changing. Even the paths are lost, but love neither fades, nor changes, nor does it ever get lost. It always stays alive. It continuously keeps going on.

Avni stood up and walked ahead while Akash followed her. They walked towards the side where Akash had stood a while back, before Avni had called him from Sakhi's phone. After going a little further, Avni stopped and turned back towards Akash.

"We may not meet again, but I will always treasure these moments. I may not be able to experience anything like this ever again." And her eyes gazed at Akash as if she wanted to absorb him completely in her.

"You have given me such precious moments today. I will keep them alive within me forever." Akash said caressing Avni with his gaze.

Avni looked away from Akash's face, pointing to the big rock with her hand and said, "There she is, waiting for you."

Akash saw that Sakhi was sitting in a corner, looking at the mountains. Her back was towards them. The sun had begun to set in the far horizon, where the pale red color was slowly spreading high in the sky. Akash stared at the waning sunlight for a while and then turned towards Avni.

However, Avni had already left from there. He could see her figure grow smaller as she kept walking away. Akash wanted to call out her name but stayed silent after giving it a thought. He quietly waved goodbye to her, looking at her till she disappeared. Then he stayed for two seconds and walked towards Sakhi.

He went and sat beside Sakhi, keeping his eyes on the setting sun. She looked at him carefully and then turned her gaze back at the setting sun. Akash placed his hand on her hand. Sakhi kept looking at the sun without moving, then she rested her head on Akash's shoulder. The pale red color of setting sun and soft floating clouds were painting the landscape in dreamy shades, while some of those colors had splashed and lit up their eyes. There the sun was parting from the sky to rest in the lap of earth and here Sakhi was blushing in Akash's embrace.